The Amazing Maddie Sykes

Linton Darling

www.LintonDarling.com
@LintonDarling

Cover illustration by John Protheroe

This book is written in British English

For an amazing girl

1.

Have you ever felt like you were invisible? Like you could go right up to someone and wave your hands in their face without them seeing a thing? Or walk through a crowded room without a single person noticing?

Me too.

For me though, it wasn't just a feeling.

School was done for the day, and I was lying on my bed staring at the ceiling. Sometimes I'm happy enough to just lie there doing nothing for hours, and this was one of those times. I'd had a rough week and I needed to shut down for a while. My bedroom ceiling had been inexpertly papered by my dad a few years back, and my eyes lazily traced the irregular patterns his efforts had left me with.

I probably hadn't moved an inch for about twenty minutes when a fly buzzed past my face, too close for comfort. I jerked my arm out in an attempt to swat it, then gave a yelp of surprise. My arm had passed right in front of my eyes, near enough for me to feel a faint waft of air against my cheeks – but I hadn't seen it.

I immediately brought both hands up to my face, shaking them frantically, but again nothing obstructed my view of the ceiling. Dropping my hands back to the bed I lay still for a moment, fighting a rising wave of panic. What was happening? Was I paralyzed, and actually my arms weren't moving at all? Or was I dead, was this what it felt like? I don't freak out easily, I'm normally a very calm person, but things were going wrong for me lately and for a moment I struggled to get on top of the situation.

"This is crazy, you are not dead," I said out loud, and felt a slight sense of relief at the sound of my own voice, which seemed to confirm my words. I swung my legs off the bed, pulling myself upright. Then I looked downwards, fearing the worst, and there was nothing to be seen – no sign of my legs, my stomach or anything else. Looking closer I could just make out an indentation in the covers beneath me, which seemed to correspond roughly to the shape of my backside, not that I had ever paid it that much attention before.

Taking a deep breath I reminded myself that I'm not a panicker. I always keep it together. "Work

3

through it," I told myself, and tried to organise my thoughts. I love using checklists whenever I have difficult things to deal with, so I created one in my head. Point one – I'm definitely not dead, which is a huge positive. I couldn't resist a smile despite the bizarre situation, picturing myself writing that down on my list with a big tick against it.

1. *Confirm that I'm not dead* ✓

If I was some sort of ghost I wouldn't be making an imprint on my duvet, I was pretty sure of that. So, what else did I know? My voice sounded normal enough. Moving my arms and waggling my feet also felt normal, aside from the small detail that I couldn't see them. I poked various parts of my body with my fingers, and they all seemed to feel the contact in the usual way too. While poking my arms it occurred to me that it wasn't just my body I couldn't see, but also my clothes. It was very unsettling to feel the texture of my cotton shirt between my fingers when my eyes were telling me there was nothing there.

For some reason the impulse struck me to check if I could still feel pain in the normal way, and I slapped myself across the cheek, quite hard. Yep, turned out I could still feel pain.

Standing up, I cautiously walked around my room. You wouldn't think having invisible feet would affect something as basic as walking, would you? Well, at first it was amazingly difficult. I banged into things, felt a bit dizzy, and nearly went flying after tripping over the sparkly Indian-style embroidered footstool my mum had assured me would look very elegant amongst my things. I guess it was a bit like travel sickness – my brain was struggling to cope with the contradictory information from my eyes and my legs. Once I'd slowed down and focused on just looking ahead of me instead of down at my missing limbs, I started to get the hang of it, and after a couple of minutes I felt like I had pretty much nailed walking – go me!

I used my newfound ability to go to my dressing table, and looked in the oval mirror mounted there. I'm not sure what I was expecting, but what I saw was absolutely nothing. Well – I saw my room, but I wasn't in it. My mind jumped straight to *Alice Through the Looking-Glass*, one of my favourite books, and I watched my collection of stuffed toys for a moment to see if they might come to life like Alice's chess pieces, and take me on a series of charming adventures. Sadly, they remained stubbornly lifeless – even my cuddly Cheshire Cat.

"OK," I thought, determined to continue with my cool-headed and logical assessment of what was happening to me. "I've established that I can't see myself, but what about other people, can they see me? And actually, can I see them? Whatever this is, maybe it's happening to everyone."

I crossed to the other side of my room and tried to open the door, but missed the handle with my invisible hand and ended up pushing it closed instead. This was clearly going to take some getting used to. I forced myself to slow down, despite every instinct telling me to hurry, and carefully felt along the door until I had located the brass handle and turned it. Stepping out onto the landing, I called out, "Mum? Dad? Are you there?"

There was no answer; the house was in complete silence except for the faint hum of the aging boiler downstairs. That was weird – one of my parents would normally be home by now. Frustrated in my plan to find out if they could see me, I went to the front bedroom and peeked through the curtains. Life outside our house seemed to carrying on as normal: cars whizzed by with a blatant disregard for the 30mph speed limit, a surprisingly large number of pigeons lounged around in our neighbour's tree, and an occasional jogger or mum with a baby buggy made their way along the path just twenty feet from where I stood. One thing was for sure, I could tick off another point on my mental checklist: I'd found that other people (and pigeons) were just as visible as ever. Could they see me though? A man I vaguely recognised wandered past with a shopping bag, and I waved frantically but he didn't look up.

"Doesn't prove anything," I reasoned to myself. "He might just not have noticed, he looked quite lost in his thoughts."

My mind drifted for a moment as I wondered what he had been thinking about. Sometimes it feels strange to think that every other person you see in the street has their own thoughts racing around in their heads, which probably seem very important to them. That guy might have been thinking about his shopping, or wondering why there are no green mammals, or planning a murder – I would never know. I wished I could tell what people were thinking, but perhaps it would all be nonsense, or nasty, or just really, really dull.

"One thing's for sure," I thought with a smile, "there probably aren't many people standing around trying to work out whether or not they're invisible."

I considered going outside, but something held me back. I wanted to get a better grip on what was going on before I risked that. Luckily, just then I saw my dad's black car pull onto the drive. He stopped the engine and then just sat at the wheel for a minute or two before slowly opening the door and ambling towards the house, somehow taking a moment to find his keys even though he had just used them to lock the car. Mum always says Dad does everything in slow motion, but even by his low standards he seemed to move at a snail's pace. I wondered whether there was any reason he wouldn't be glad to be home, but quickly dismissed the thought.

"You're experiencing something that's never happened before in the whole of human history, probably the scariest thing that will ever happen in your life, so let's just focus on that shall we?" I chastised myself. "If Dad's in a bad mood about something then... well, that's his problem frankly, under the circumstances. I'm frickin' invisible here! I need to know if he can see me."

Hearing Dad move into the kitchen, I decided to creep downstairs so I could see how things stood without having to actually ask the crazy question, "Am I invisible?"

I made my way down very carefully, stepping on the outsides of each step rather than the middle so they wouldn't creak. Learning the lessons from my attempts at walking around my bedroom, I kept my focus in front of me so that I wouldn't be put off by not seeing my feet, and managed to negotiate my way to the hallway as silently as I'd hoped. Moving to the open kitchen door, I peeped around the corner and saw my dad sitting at the small wooden kitchen table. He had one hand propped under his chin and was staring listlessly at the fridge, right next to the doorway.

"This is it," I thought to myself, taking a deep breath and stepping forward to stand on the kitchen tiles in front of him. I'm not sure what I expected, but Dad's gaze didn't even flicker; he carried on looking right through me at the fridge, with a blank expression on his face. I waved my arms around, and even attempted a little dance before realising my feet were making a shuffling sound on the floor that might give me away. I needn't have worried though – Dad didn't notice a thing.

I turned and softly retreated back to my room, having learned two things: firstly, my dad had a worrying obsession with a kitchen appliance, and secondly… I really was invisible!

2.

Back in my room, I sat down on my bed with my head in my hands and felt a wave of hopelessness wash over me. Was this my life now, would I stay like this forever?

"I'm supposed to be going shopping with Lucy at the weekend, that's going to be a waste of time," I thought bitterly, and felt an unseen tear roll down my nose. A moment later though, I found myself laughing at my own self-pity. Something incredible was happening to me, something life-changing, and I was worrying about missing out on an hour or two of shopping.

I forced myself to start thinking logically again, and focused my attention on the most important question facing me: could I become visible again? I had no idea what I had done, if anything, to bring about this strange transformation, so how could I reverse it?

My first step was to lie back on the bed in the exact position I had been in before. Remembering that my eyes had been roaming over the patterns on my ceiling, I tried to recreate the path my gaze had taken, stopping every few seconds to check my arms for any signs that they might be miraculously reappearing. When this didn't work, I tried following the pattern backwards, reasoning that this would be more likely to counteract the effects, but without success.

Then I remembered the fly - maybe it had something to do with all this. I searched my room without finding it, and was on the point of giving up when I heard a faint buzzing noise coming from the other side of the blinds. Quietly moving over towards my window, I saw the fly sitting on the glass, rubbing its front legs together in a way I've always found really unpleasant. So, I'd tracked it down, what now? For some reason I tried to communicate with it mentally, fixing it with an intense stare and thinking the words, "Please make me visible!" as clearly as I could.

The fly didn't react. It seemed to be looking at me with its bulbous red eyes, but that might just have been a coincidence. Feeling slightly embarrassed despite the fact that I was both:

A) on my own

and

B) invisible

… I gave up on the psychic approach and whispered, "Hello?"

This time the fly gave a response of sorts, stopping the hand-rubbing thing and shifting its position slightly. Encouraged, I went on, "Please can you make me visible?"

Nothing. The fly remained completely motionless. A thought occurred to me: flies were one of the few living things I would ever willingly kill, along with mosquitoes, my rationale being that they had the capability to harm humans through the spread of disease and as such were our natural enemies. Could it be that this was like one of those stories where the main character suffers terrible punishments that can only be ended when they learn the error of their ways and become a better person? You know, like in *Beauty and the Beast* or *Freaky Friday*. Thinking for a second, I decided to lay it on thick.

"Oh, noble fly," I whispered, "I have wronged your people. Well, not people, but flies. You know what I mean. You have done me no harm, but on several occasions I have harmed or even killed your brethren. When I say you've done me no harm, I should say in my defence that you have pulled some slightly shady moves, like walking in my food… but that's all in the past now. As I said, I have wronged you, and I apologise. I swear to you that from this moment on, I will never harm another fly as long as I live."

Having concluded my speech, I waited, hardly daring to breathe, as the fly considered my words. Or at least that's what I hoped it was doing. It carried on staring impassively in my direction, certainly. After perhaps a minute, it turned and walked upwards towards the top of the window-pane, ending up with its back to me.

I lost my patience, and throwing caution to the wind I shouted, "Damn it, fly! Turn me back to how I was RIGHT NOW!"

I slammed my hand against the wooden slats of the blind, and the fly got scared and started frantically flying into the window, taking a face full of glass each time. The noise obviously distracted my dad from his contemplation of the fridge door, because he called up, "Maddie? Is that you? Are you okay?"

"I'm fine, Dad, be down in a bit," I replied, cursing myself for making such a commotion. I calmed down, and the fly did too, settling back on its original spot in the middle of the window. At this point another idea occurred to me – the fly might well have been responsible for my disappearance, and I'd tried all peaceful means to resolve the situation. Perhaps, in some strange way, this insect represented a trial I had to overcome, like one of the twelve tasks of Hercules – most of which ended with him killing something.

As if sensing the danger that the direction of my thoughts placed it in, the fly chose that moment to take off and buzz around the room for a minute or two, eventually landing on my door. I advanced stealthily towards it, determined to end its life without compassion if it meant me becoming visible again. Standing before it, something stayed my hand: not any last minute qualms about crushing a fellow creature, simply the fact that squashing a fly with your fingers is a bit icky. Looking around for something I could use, nothing leapt out at me, so I lifted a foot and yanked my sock off, intending to use it as a weapon.

To my surprise, the moment the sock left my foot it popped into view, as if by magic. I held it in front of my face and it just hung there, looking faintly ridiculous suspended in mid-air. Now this was interesting, and encouraging: it was obviously possible for something to go from being invisible back to visible – that had to be good news.

I hesitated for a moment, wondering whether I should explore this new angle a little further or deal with the fly first. If I could control the visibility of my sock just by taking it off, surely I could find a way to get the same control over my whole body, couldn't I? Then again – what if killing the fly really was the key to undoing whatever freaky witchcraft had left me in this state? What if I let it go, and it found its way out of the house, never to be seen again? I couldn't take that chance.

Slowly extending my arm, I got into position to swat my adversary. I was a one-girl swat team. I'd found in the past that flies can be incredibly good at dodging just at the last second when you think you've got them, and I thought to myself, "I wish my sock was still invisible, so the fly wouldn't see it coming."

As I finished this thought, the sock momentarily took on a slightly glassy, translucent appearance, before returning to normal a second later. I paused again, granting another stay of execution for my oblivious nemesis. Did I do that? I slowly tried to think the exact same thought again: "I wish my sock was still invisible." This time nothing happened, and the offending garment dangled defiantly before me looking more solid than ever.

Maybe I needed to crank up the volume. "I WISH IT WAS INVISIBLE!" I shouted internally. It sounded strange for my normally calm inner voice to be raised like that, and it was no surprise to find it didn't work. Going the other way, I closed my eyes, took a deep breath, and imagined myself softly whispering, "I wish it was invisible," while picturing the sock slowly fading from sight.

I tentatively opened one eye, then tried to suppress a squeak of excitement; the sock had vanished! I could still feel it between my fingers, but it was just as imperceptible as it had been when I was wearing it. I hugged myself with joy, finally feeling there was some grounds for optimism about my situation. Perhaps if I used the same approach I could restore myself to normal, and this whole thing would be over.

I gave a rueful chuckle at the thought of how down I'd been just a few minutes earlier, and the crazy plans I'd tried in order to become visible again. Now I felt like things were going my way, and there was light at the end of the tunnel. Still, best not to count your chickens before they're hatched, so I crushed the fly into a messy pulp against my door, just in case.

3.

Sitting back down on my bed, I took a deep breath, closed my eyes and tried to clear my mind. Without any words this time, I pictured my body slowly reappearing, starting from my feet and working upwards. When I reached my waist I had a moment of panic: I couldn't actually remember which top I had on – did that matter? In my mind's eye, I flipped between several items in my wardrobe, picturing myself in each one and then discarding it. Would whatever I imagined myself wearing suddenly appear? Wait – what if I imagined something really bad, would that appear?

"Well, let's just not do that, problem solved," I told myself, but I'd no sooner made that resolution than my imagination plucked out the image of myself covered from the waist up not by clothes, but by a seething mass of wasps. With a shudder of revulsion I snapped my eyes open and looked down. No nightmarish wasp swarm greeted me, just a minor disappointment. My legs were there, looking completely normal as they hung over the edge of the bed, but above them was no more than the faint outline of my stomach, chest, and arms. As I watched, my legs began to fade again, and within moments I was back to square one, better concealed than the stealthiest ninja.

"Come on!" I urged myself. "You're just invisible, you're not God – wasps are not going to appear from nowhere just because you imagine them."

I needed to focus. To avoid a repeat of my previous failure, the first thing to do was remember what I was wearing. I cast my mind back to when I got home from school. It must only have been an hour or two but it felt like a lifetime ago. I'd been a bit pre-occupied with other things, and I guess I got changed on auto-pilot – I had no recollection at all of what I'd put on. I ran my fingers over my sleeves and torso, and came across something that felt like letters printed on my chest. I traced out a "C"… "H"…. of course! It had to be my grey Chicago Bears sweater. It was one of my favourites for lounging around at home even though my dad, as a Green Bay Packers fan, objected to it. I'd explained to him a hundred times that I have no interest in sports and I'd bought it simply because I like bears, but he still gave me a mournful look every time I wore it.

I closed my eyes and tried again, feeling confident I had a good mental image of myself this time. Deep breaths – start from the feet – work upwards to the waist – picture the Bears logo appearing on my chest – then up towards my neck – onto the face, including all the freckles – finish with my hair... done. I paused for a moment then cautiously peaked down at the results. Legs, stomach, arms, hands: they were all back! I rushed to the mirror, and there looking back at me was my face, grinning like an idiot. I never would have believed I could be so happy to see my own reflection, under any circumstances, but I felt a moment of complete euphoria and found myself prancing around the room, racing back now and again to double-check that every detail of my appearance was just as it had been before.

I stared deeply into my greeny-blue eyes, stuck out my tongue, wrinkled my nose, even checked the filling in one of my molars; everything was just at it used to be. "I'll never take you for granted again," I told my face, as it looked back at me with a serious expression. You always take things for granted until they're taken away from you though, don't you? It's human nature. You think something will always be there for you until suddenly – BANG! – it's gone.

When the thrill of seeing myself again started to wear off, I began to wonder if I would disappear again. Did I want to? Now that I had no fears of being stuck in my ghost-like state forever, I considered for the first time what fun it might be if I could turn invisible whenever I wanted.

"I'd be crazy not to at least check if I can do it," I resolved, and set about the task quickly before any nagging doubts could creep in. I closed my eyes again, and pictured myself disappearing. For some reason it seemed to make sense to work from the head down this time, finishing off with my toes. Opening my eyes a few seconds later, I was pleased to see nothing but my fluffy pink rug when I looked down towards where my legs should be; I was really getting the hang of this!

I ran through the process a few more times, appearing and disappearing as quickly as I could. I soon had the transition down to about five seconds, as long as nothing distracted me. Satisfied that I had mastered this amazing new skill, I then set about trying to understand how it worked a little better. Remembering my experience with the sock earlier, I tried picking up other things and making them disappear. This was slightly less successful – I started with my chair, then my laptop, then moved on to my school bag. All three items stubbornly refused to vanish, although I got a momentary glassy flicker from the bag. "Might be something to do with how heavy they are," I reflected, and grabbed the stuffed Cheshire Cat. I focused really hard on imagining it fading from view, starting with the tip of its tail and finishing (of course) with its broad grin. To my delight this had the desired effect, and the cat dangled invisibly from my hand until I let it slip through my fingers, at which point it promptly popped back into view.

The next thing I was curious to find out was whether I could be seen by electronic devices. Grabbing my phone I took a series of selfies, fading in and out as I did so. As I suspected, the camera couldn't see me any better than the human eye: half the pictures showed nothing more than the empty room behind me. For a second I considered sending one of the images to Lucy, my best friend, but I immediately realised how ridiculous that would look – a picture of my bedroom wall with, "OMG, I can turn invisible!" as the caption. She'd just think it was some lame joke. I couldn't wait to tell her about all this – she'd be so excited – but the whole "I now have an incredible power the likes of which the world has never seen" conversation was going to have to be face-to-face.

At this point I felt a call of nature, and inevitably my mind turned to bathroom matters, and how my new situation would affect… all that. It's gross, but I have to admit I was more than a little fascinated to see what would happen as I went through to the toilet, sat down, and quickly faded myself away. Looking down, I could see straight into the toilet bowl below me. It was relatively clean for once – Dad must have done that weird thing where he cleans it using a bottle of Coke. I felt something coming, and watched as… well, I don't really need to describe it in detail. Suffice to say it wasn't a pleasurable experience: one star out of five, would not recommend to a friend.

Making my way back to my room afterwards, a thought suddenly occurred to me: I'd mastered the whole invisibility thing, but what if that wasn't the only strange gift I was blessed with? Perhaps I could do other incredible things if I put my mind to them. I'd often had a conversation with Lucy about which superpower we would have if we could choose; Lucy always said time travel, but for me it was a no-brainer... it had to be the ability to fly.

"Tricky one to test," I mused, looking around my bedroom for inspiration. My eyes were drawn to the window for a second before common sense prevailed. "Nope, let's not make 'Turns out I can't fly' my dying words," I decided. "Let's start small."

I clambered onto my bed and started bouncing. It's an Ikea special, not especially bouncy, but I could still get nearly a second of hang time on each bounce. Assuming my technique for becoming invisible might work to get me airborne, I closed my eyes and pictured myself reaching the top of my leap and then just not coming back down. To my annoyance, gravity rudely ignored my efforts and pulled me back down to earth with frustrating consistency. I stopped to think for a moment. Another of my favourite books was *Peter Pan*, and I brought to mind the instructions for flight that Peter explained to

Wendy and her brothers. "Basically it's all about happy thoughts," I recalled, choosing to ignore the fact that fairy dust was also a big part of the process. I started bouncing again and tried to fill my mind with a happy thought. For some reason nothing came instantly to mind. I tried to remember something that had made me happy in the last few days, but I came up empty – how depressing!

I cast my recollections further back, and a silly memory popped into my head. I was in Austria, on holiday with my parents, years ago. My dad had gone to get us chocolate ice creams from a gelato stand, but in the intense midday sun they had started to melt almost immediately. By the time he got back to where Mum and I were sitting, the melted chocolate had run down both his arms to the elbows, and dripped from there down his legs. He looked like he was staging a dirty protest of some sort, and urgently held out the ice creams for us to take. Mum found the spectacle hilarious and refused to take hers, forcing him to hold on to it until he was thoroughly covered in brown, sticky goop. We laughed at him until our sides hurt, drawing the attention of people nearby and thus adding to Dad's discomfort and our amusement. He took it in reasonably good spirits though, and eventually trudged off to dispose of the now inedible treats.

It was a slightly weird happy thought, I suppose, but it was certainly a vivid memory – I could picture Mum laughing, the bench we were sitting on, and the sparkling lake in front of us as clearly as if it happened yesterday. Focusing on those images I closed my eyes, spread my arms wide, and flung myself upwards from the bed, out towards the middle of the room.

I came down hard. Having been convinced it would work, I didn't protect myself against the impact until the last second, and landed heavily on my hands and knees. A searing pain shot through my wrists and I wondered for a second if I'd broken them. Luckily my thick fluffy rug had broken my fall a little, leaving me with nothing worse than the beginnings of some nasty bruises.

I heard footsteps hurrying across the hallway downstairs, and Dad called up again, "Maddie, is everything alright up there?"

"Yep… just moving my furniture around," I called back, my teeth gritted in pain. Gingerly getting back on my feet, I had a half-hearted attempt at trying out some other powers. I tried to stop time, teleport, lift my bed with one hand, and finally shoot fireballs from my hands – all without success. Kind of lucky that last one didn't work actually, as I realised afterwards I had been aiming at my underwear drawer.

"Looks like it's just the invisibility then," I thought to myself. *Just invisibility.* Just an incredible superpower which any normal person would kill for! I took a moment to appreciate that, and the fact that this strange phenomenon might end as suddenly as it began. I needed to make full use of it, but how?

If I was in a comic book I'd use my new ability to fight crime and save the world from terrible enemies, but was that a realistic goal for me? My home town didn't have that many criminals, as far as I knew, so if I wanted to fight crime I'd have to go somewhere else... London, perhaps? But London's so big – how would I know where a crime was going to happen? Plus, not all crimes are the kind of thing an invisible person can easily prevent. I wasn't going to be able to do much about a fight breaking out in the street, or a person drink-driving and crashing their car into a pedestrian. At the other end of the spectrum, if some sort of "Doctor Evil" came up with a plan to attach rocket boosters to the moon and crash it into Belgium, again it was hard to imagine I could do much to help.

I parked the idea of fighting crime, and thought about a less noble way to use my power: becoming rich and famous. In some ways this seemed more promising; a girl who could disappear would be huge news, surely. I could go on a TV talent show to get my name out there as a magician, and then when I had the world's attention I could reveal that this was no cheap trick but real magic. I'd become famous overnight, every talk show in the country would want the real live Invisible Girl as a guest, and then maybe I could have my own show: *Maddie Sykes Live.* I would design my own clothing line, maybe with transparent fabric – that could be my gimmick. I'd become the most famous person in the world, and probably have to move to a big house with tall fences just to keep all my fans away. I guess I'd have to leave school, maybe study at home…

The picture of my life as a leading celebrity began to lose a little of its lustre, and another concern occurred to me: it wouldn't just be fans queuing up outside my fences. What would the military give to understand the secret of becoming invisible? An army with my powers would be unstoppable. Not just the military either – what about terrorists, or gangsters? I imagined a ruthless gang kidnapping my parents, and forcing me to steal the crown jewels to secure their release.

This was a worrying thought. I scratched the idea of fame and fortune, at least for now. "I don't have to plan everything out this instant," I decided. "It might not even last that long. I definitely don't need to rush into telling the world just yet, I need to be a bit careful. I have to tell someone though! This is so huge, it would be impossible to just keep it to myself."

Who to tell though? I could have gone downstairs right then and talked to my dad, but something held me back. Things had been weird between us lately, and we just weren't in that place where I could share something like this. Eventually

I settled on Lucy. It had been my first instinct to tell her, and I knew she'd be super excited, perhaps with a hint of jealousy on the side. I'd certainly be envious if it was the other way around. The only challenge would be getting her to keep my secret: she was a chatterbox at the best of times, and giving her something this big but then trying to stop her shouting it from the roof of the school hall would be tough. On balance though, I felt like I could trust her with it, and resolved to confide in her the next day.

I smiled in eager anticipation of the scene; her disbelief turning to astonishment as I demonstrated what I could do. My one fear was that I might lose my new talent when I fell asleep that night, so after dinner I spent a good couple of hours flicking between my visible and invisible states, trying to somehow embed the process indelibly in my mind. It was surprisingly tiring, and by 10pm I was ready to drop. I flopped down on my bed without even getting changed, disappeared myself one last time for luck, then fell into a deep, dreamless sleep.

4.

As I woke up, my mind did its usual warm up routine. "What's that noise – isn't it the middle of the night? Nope, looks like it's morning. How can it be morning already, didn't I fall asleep like 12 seconds ago? Okay, okay, it really is morning. Is it at least the weekend? No, can't be, my alarm wouldn't be going off. It's probably one of those pathetic, meaningless days like Wednesday or Thursday. Or Tuesday. Anything happening today? Anything out of the…."

Suddenly my consciousness kicked in fully, and I sat bolt upright without finishing that rambling thought. Yes, there was something out of the ordinary about today. Today was my second day as a person who could turn invisible, and would be the day I showed someone else my new trick for the first time. Or would it? I looked down at my hands and arms. They looked as normal as ever: the very picture of standard, unexceptional hands, attached to arms which were, if anything, even more average. I had a moment of uncertainty.

"Please, please don't give me any of that 'it was all a dream' nonsense," I told my hands sternly, as if they were deliberately putting doubts in my mind. I knew there was nothing imaginary about yesterday's miraculous events – I could still feel a faint pain in my cheek from where I slapped myself, and look! Over there on my door were the remains of the unfortunate fly. This comforted me a little, but it was with some trepidation that I took a deep breath, closed my eyes and repeated the process that had worked so well the day before.

I needn't have worried. Within a second, it was over. Gone were the slow transitions of my earliest attempts; I hardly needed to keep my eyes closed for longer than a blink to completely vanish. I blinked in and out a dozen times, hugging myself with glee now that I could set aside my worst fear – losing my power in my sleep.

Now I couldn't wait to tell Lucy, and I hurried through breakfast and getting ready for school. I found myself singing in the shower, like I always used to do whenever I was happy. "When was the last time I did this?" I wondered, as I came to the end of one of my favourite songs. "You can grow out of things, I guess... but not being happy, surely?" I never dwell on unpleasant thoughts, so I discarded that line of enquiry and rushed on with drying and dressing myself.

Dad was being even slower than usual, taking an age to find his keys as I waited impatiently at the front door. Eventually we made it out of the house and got to school with a minute or two to spare. Lucy was near the front gates, talking to Sophia and Amy and rattling off a hundred words a minute in her usual way. She gave me a friendly wave and I joined them, trying to subtly hint with a contortion of my eyebrows that I wanted a word with her in private. Unfortunately Lucy doesn't really deal in subtleties, and instead of taking the hint she started copying me, waggling her eyebrows in a comically exaggerated manner as she spoke. The others couldn't help but notice this, and after much good natured teasing it quickly turned into a contest to see who could pull the most ridiculous face. I reluctantly joined in and was eventually declared the winner by my friends, facial expressions being one of my particular talents – just not the one I had been intending to share that morning.

Before I could come up with another way to drag Lucy away to have "the conversation", the bell rang and we were forced to join the stream of students hurrying in to class. When we had taken our usual places next to each other at registration, I whispered, "What are you doing at lunchtime? I need to talk to you about something – it's important."

"Oh... really sorry but I promised Mr Chopra I would polish the fencing swords this lunchtime," she replied.

"Can't that wait? Maybe do it tomorrow? This is really important."

"Sorry, Maddie, but I did promise him, and you know what teachers are like – he'll be writing to my parents if I let him down."

I considered this unlikely; Lucy was the star of the fencing team, based on a potent combination of her towering height and wild enthusiasm. There was no way Mr Chopra would hold it against his best pupil if she delayed helping him out by one day. Still, she was dead set on doing it, so I bit my tongue and didn't urge her any further. "I guess we can talk later," I said.

"Sure, yeah, we'll definitely catch up later," she assured me, giving my arm a squeeze.

As it turned out I barely saw Lucy for the rest of the day. I ate my lunch alone, feeling unable to join in with the usual lunchtime gossip with my other friends, and in the afternoon we had language lessons which meant Spanish for me while Lucy had French in the classroom down the hall.

After school we usually had ten or fifteen minutes to kill while we waited for our parents to pick us up. Sometimes we walked to the nearby shops, but today I figured there might be more time to share my huge news if we just waited by the school gates. In my eagerness, I dashed out of the building as soon as the final bell rang, well ahead of most of my class. I took a seat on the bench by the bus stop, and began to rehearse the conversation with Lucy in my head as I watched for her to appear.

"Lucy, I've got something immense to tell you: I have a superpower," I imagined myself saying. I smiled at the very thought of saying those words, but then forced the grin off my face. I needed a serious expression so she would believe me. Maybe I should word it a bit differently.

"Lucy, don't tell anyone, but I can disappear."

"What, move to Peru like you always talked about? Why would you do that – have you killed someone? Have you finally snapped and murdered Liza Preston? Or stolen Miss Parker's false teeth?" I imagined her responding.

There was no real likelihood of me committing the crimes in question, despite the fact that Liza Preston was the most evil girl in our year, while the idea of swiping our headmistress's dentures was one we had often discussed. It was almost inevitable that Lucy's lively imagination would turn in these directions. I gave a sigh; it wasn't going to be easy to get this right. Probably best to just show her what I could do, if we could find somewhere out of sight.

As I was turning this over in my mind, I saw Lucy walking towards me. She was deep in conversation with Sophia as they approached the school gates, just across the road from where I was sitting. I gave them a wave, but they didn't notice me, so I got up and waved my arms around like a crazy person, jumping up and down on the spot as I did so. Lucy and I often do stuff like that; it's a point of pride and a cornerstone of our friendship that we never let embarrassment stop us from playing around like five-year-olds.

To my surprise though, Lucy and Sophia didn't seem to see me – they came out of the gates, passed within a few yards from me, and turned left towards the shops, intent on their conversation. "Lucy!" I tried to call out, but my voice failed me and it came out little louder than a whisper. Why would they have ignored me like that? They must have seen me…

A thought crossed my mind and I looked down, where I saw nothing but concrete paving slabs and a couple of cigarette butts. Once again, no sign of my feet, legs, or anything else. I gasped in surprise, then put my hand over my mouth, suddenly terrified of anyone hearing me. How had this happened? I thought I had it completely under control, after those hours of practice the previous night. What would make me disappear without even trying?

"I can't think about it now," I resolved hurriedly, "I need to 'blink in' again before Mum arrives to collect me, and I can't do it here in the street – it's way too busy."

I looked around. Superman always found a convenient phone booth to get changed in, but you don't see a lot of those near my school. Anyway, even if there was one right next to me it would be hard to get into without anyone seeing the door open. The only option that presented itself was a little group of bushes set a few feet back from the bench I was sitting on. Not ideal because they were only waist-high, but I didn't feel like I had a lot of choice. More children were wandering through the gates towards the bus stop, and the longer I left it the more likely it was that someone would trip over me or, even worse, sit on me.

I got up and carefully made my way over to the bushes, as quietly as I could, weaving around a little kid from the year below me who had just arrived, casually throwing his school bag on the path just in front of me. Some older children sauntered over too, and a chunky girl whose name I could never remember lowered her substantial weight right onto the spot I'd been sitting a moment earlier – I'd had a narrow escape. Wasting no more time, I

ducked down behind the bushes. I found they of-
fered a disappointingly low quality of cover: not
only were they lacking in height, but their branches
were also quite spindly and didn't provide the level
of concealment I wanted. Giving a quiet growl of
frustration, I lay flat on the ground and rolled over
until I was as close as I could get to the base of the
biggest plant. Down here I felt reasonably sure none
of the growing horde of kids around the bench could
see me, so I took a moment to gain some composure,
then blinked myself back to full visibility.

As soon as I'd done a quick check of my arms
and legs to make sure I hadn't left myself with an
invisible thumb or anything crazy like that, I got to
my feet, wondering if Lucy was going to come back
this way. Some older boys were standing nearby,
and one of them nudged the others, who turned
around to look at me. Some of them smirked at my
appearance, and I realised too late that I probably
did look a bit strange; from their perspective I had

simply been lying in a bush, and I now had a gener-ous coating of mud and a few twigs in my hair as a result.

"Like it in the bush, do ya?" enquired Leon Langford, a short, blond kid who was considered quite a comedian by his simple-minded friends. Some of them confirmed this with sniggers as he spoke. I ignored him, just like adults always tell you to do, and walked back towards the bench.

"Come back and tell us what's so great about your bush!"

More sniggers.

"You're a bush freak! With stick hair!"

I almost had to smile at his inability to do more with the fairly solid materials for a witty insult I had presented him with, but I forced my face to stay impassive to avoid encouraging him. At that moment another boy from their class came over and threw an arm around Leon's neck in a friendly head lock, ruffling his gelled blond hair. "Not your best smack-talk bro," he said. "Give her a break, though – she's just a kid."

The newcomer was Jake White, who lived just a few houses away on my street. I'd known him since I was a toddler, and though we didn't spend much time together anymore I still thought of him as a friend. Leon wriggled out of his grip angrily, and was about to respond when Jake pulled him in close and leant down to whisper something in his ear. Leon's eyes flicked towards me a couple of times as Jake spoke, and afterwards he shrugged and turned away. Soon the boys were talking about football and I was apparently forgotten.

This little encounter left me with mixed feelings. I appreciated Jake's intervention, but it hurt a little to hear myself dismissed as "just a kid". If only he knew what this kid could do, he might label me a little differently! And what had he whispered to Leon? Something else about how I wasn't even worth the effort of mocking, perhaps? Still, I quickly put the whole thing behind me – it was hardly the most pressing thing on my mind, after all. I looked around for Lucy again, but she still hadn't come back from the shops and within a few minutes my parents' car rolled into view to collect me.

5.

I got home feeling super frustrated. How could the whole day have gone past without me getting a chance to tell Lucy about what was going on? Stomping up to my room, I lay on my bed and tried my normal technique for dealing with one of life's disappointments: pushing it to the back of my mind and forgetting about it. With this goal in mind I read for a while, watched some old sitcoms on my tablet, got out my sketchpad and began drawing a picture of a badger, even went down and sorted out the re-cycling, which is normally Mum's job – anything to take my mind off invisibility for a while.

Back in my room, I got out my diary and flipped to the most recent entry. It was from about two weeks back, when apparently my major concern had been whether to get my hair cut a lot shorter, going from halfway down my back to maybe shoul-der length. In the end I hadn't done it. I wrote in the date and then paused, my pen hovering over the page. This should have been the perfect way to deal with my annoyance over not being able to share my amazing news with anyone, but something was making me hesitate. Fear of someone else reading it, perhaps? That didn't really make sense because there was a lot of very personal info in this diary that was for my eyes only – I also had a great hiding place for it under a loose floorboard, so there was no rea-son to suspect anyone else would ever see it. Still, for some reason I felt reluctant to commit words to the page. Eventually, with an effort, I simply wrote, "I'm becoming invisible," then slammed the book shut and stowed it away.

I grabbed my phone and started playing a game, but I soon realised I was wasting my time: there was no way I could focus on anything else until I'd spoken to Lucy and told her my secret. I killed the game and made a call to Lucy. She didn't pick up, but I knew how she never has her phone with her and can never find it when it rings, so I stuck with it. After maybe five minutes of failed calls, the icon on my phone turned green and Lucy's face appeared, her wide smile filling the screen.

"Hey Maddie! What's up? Are your teeth on fire?"

It was our tradition to start our calls with an exchange of wildly improbable questions, but on this occasion I wanted to strike a more serious tone so she would know I wasn't joking when I told her my news.

"No, my teeth are fine," I replied briskly. "How's things with you?"

"Awesome, thanks. So – oh my god – you know what happened in French earlier? Justin, you know, the kid that always wears that green hoodie, he was trying to ask directions to the train station, in French obviously, but you know how he has that stammer, so he's all, '*Ou-ou-ou-ou est la ga-ga-gare?*' and Liza Preston, you know what a little beast that she can be, she was rolling her eyes and making fun of him, and then when it was her turn she said '*J'ai quarante ans,*' which means 'I am forty' – hah! Isn't that typical Liza? Don't know why she thinks she's so special. I felt really sorry for Justin, he's actually quite nice, but he's into, like, Dungeons and Gammon or whatever it's called. Saying that though, I like how you have all those different weird dice, with like eight sides, or ninety-seven sides... or maybe only two sides, I'm not sure. Do you like them, Maddie? Dice, but with a weird number of sides?"

"I haven't really seen them, Luce, but they sound life-changing. Listen though," I continued hurriedly, knowing I might not get a word in again for twenty minutes, "I need to talk to you about something. This is going to sound pretty crazy, but just hear me out, okay? This is not a joke, I'm totally serious."

"Yep, yep, sure – totally serious. Engaging totally serious face," Lucy replied, and I watched as she struggled without much success to force her jovial features into an uncharacteristically grave expression. Then a thought obviously occurred to her, and she asked, "Oh, is this about…?"

"It's not anything we've talked about before," I interrupted, not wanting her to go off at a tangent. "It's… well, it's news. Big news. A bit like… well, it's not like anything really, it's just big. Huge."

"News! Okay, big news, gotcha. Ready to re-ceive."

"Okay, good. So... the news is... erm... just remember that I am totally, utterly serious here... the news is that something weird happened last night, and now I can literally become invisible. Like, really, truly invisible. You can't see me. Well, not just you – nobody can... because I'm invisible."

"Right...." Lucy replied, expectantly. It was clear that despite my declarations of seriousness, she was awaiting some sort of punchline.

"That's it. That's the news, Luce. I can make myself disappear."

"Okaaaaaay... so you mean like a magic trick? That sounds cool. I didn't know you were into magic."

"No, it's not a magic trick – or at least, it might be some sort of magic, but it's not a trick, it's real."

"I understand," she replied. "It's not a trick, and you can't reveal your secrets, that's how it works in the magical world, everyone knows that."

"No – I know you're thinking I'm just messing around, but this is for real. Just watch this." I propped the phone up on my dresser, made sure I was still in view, and then quickly blinked out.

"What do you think?" I asked, after quickly checking to make sure it had worked and I was completely invisible.

"I can't see you," Lucy told me. "Turn the phone around a bit."

"No, Lucy, listen – you can't see me because I'm invisible. Look!"

I picked the phone up and swept it around the room, trying to demonstrate that I was nowhere to be seen. There was a pause, and then Lucy responded, "Oh my god, Maddie – I see what you mean, you really are invisible! And you know what's even more bizarre?"

"What? Tell me!" I asked, excited that she was finally getting it.

"I'm invisible too!"

I looked at the screen, and sure enough Lucy's face had vanished. All I could see was her room, as chaotically messy as ever.

"Luce – are you serious? Have you really disappeared too?" My heart raced at the thought of having someone to go through this experience with me. What a difference that would make – creeping around on your own without being seen was one thing, but imagine doing it with your best friend!

Sadly, my happy thoughts were crushed a second later as Lucy sprang back into view on the screen.

"Of course not, you certifiable lunatic!" she giggled. "Just imagine if we could though: imagine if we could really turn invisible. You know what I'd do? I'd just walk around the school, and every time I saw someone who's been mean to me – or you – I'd kick them right in the butt. You laughed at my hair? Kick in the butt. You ignored me when I said 'hi'? Kick in the butt. You're Liza Preston? Two kicks in the butt: one for each cheek."

"But I'm serious, this is real…"

My voice trailed off and I sighed. Lucy wasn't listening, she was still listing the people who would be in for a butt-kicking if she ever became invisible. This turned out to be a wide variety of people, ranging from children and teachers at our school to TV chefs and talent show judges, whom she was now doing an impression of.

"I loved how you were able to take a classic butt-kicking and really make it your own."

I heard a faint voice calling Lucy's name and she turned to shout back, "Just give me twelve seconds! Maddie, I've got to go, but listen: it's really good to see you, erm, back to your usual self, you know. Talk soon."

She prodded her screen to end the call, leaving me feeling deflated. There was absolutely nothing normal about what was happening to me, and I absolutely ached to share it with someone. Why was it so hard?

6.

I slumped back on my bed in a sour frame of mind. "Great, so the most amazing thing in the history of humanity happens to me and nobody even wants to hear about it," I thought, bitterly – setting aside the minor point that actually I had only tried to tell one person. Sometimes when things don't go my way I feel like the whole world is against me. Eventually I decided it was time to shove it in the face of the uncaring world and go out to enjoy my awesome new ability on my own.

I stood in front of my mirror and blinked out, taking some quiet satisfaction from being able to achieve full invisibility in less than a second. Then I crept downstairs and peeped in at the kitchen door. Dad was sitting at the table again, although he had now turned and shifted his attention from the fridge to the garden fence. Just like the day before, I was a bit surprised he would choose to spend his free time staring at inanimate objects, but I realised I was getting a rare insight into what people do when they don't know they're being watched. In this particular case what he was doing could best be described as "absolutely nothing", but it made me wonder what strange behaviour I might see from other people in my life while I was unobserved. I crept forward a bit further to see if there was anything unusual going on in the garden, and heard a faint sound as my hip brushed against the doorway. Dad must have heard it too because he glanced towards me for a second, but seeing nothing there he soon resumed his scrutiny of the fence.

Not wanting to push my luck, I carefully backed away down the hallway and let myself out of the front door as quietly as I could. Mum clearly wasn't home yet, so I knew I had a bit of time before dinner was ready and my absence might be noticed. Walking to the low wall that marked the edge of our property I hesitated, undecided as to how to take advantage of my invisibility. A few people were in view, walking up and down our street, but they were all strangers. Various pranks popped into my head, ways that I could mess with these random passers-by, but nothing really appealed – it's just not in my nature to enjoy playing practical jokes on people I don't know.

For want of a better idea, my feet began taking me in the direction of our local shop. I've been going there ever since I was a toddler and Mr Rai, the owner, always had a soft spot for me. From the age of about two upwards he's been telling my parents that I am a very intelligent girl, destined to run the country one day. I'm not sure what I've done to justify this immense belief in my abilities, but still – when I was a little kid I used to like hearing him sing my praises. What would he say if he knew I'd been blessed with this incredible gift? Probably, "I told you so."

I stopped outside the shop and peeped in through the large glass pane in the door. There was nobody behind the counter, which was not unusual; Mr Rai and his wife were often in the room at the back if there were no customers around. I eased the door open as quietly as I could, and nearly had it wide enough to slip inside when I heard the tinkling of a bell above me. I cursed under my breath – of course, there was a bell that rang when the door opened, that's how they knew they had a customer to serve. Stupid of me not to remember that when I'd been through that door a hundred times.

I quickly slipped inside and closed the door behind me, a second before Mrs Rai appeared from the back room. She looked momentarily surprised, obviously thinking it was weird that the bell had rung but there was nobody in the shop, and advanced towards me down the narrow aisle between the shelves. She went behind the little counter just in front of where I stood, and after looking straight through me and out of the shop window to the street beyond for a minute, she began absently flipping through a local paper with a look of concern on her face. I guessed business must be bad, and this was another example of how different people looked when they couldn't see me – I was used to seeing her happy and smiling whenever I came in.

Now what? I'd come out determined to enjoy my new powers, but so far I wasn't really doing much with them. Bizarrely, I got a sudden urge to steal something. "Seriously?" I questioned myself.

"Steal from lovely Mrs Rai, who looks all sad because the shop isn't doing too well?"

Despite these reproaches, I found my hand moving towards the snacks that were stacked neatly on the shelf next to me. Compromising with my conscience, I sought out the cheapest item, a little plastic box of mints. "This is important," I reasoned with myself. "Important for humanity, really. I'm the only person in the world who has this ability – I need to put it to the test and understand it better."

"… by stealing from an old lady," my conscience replied sarcastically. "Yes, you really are all about helping mankind, remember this in your speech when you win the Nobel Prize."

"Zip it!" I hissed, internally. "I'm doing this."

I gripped the mints gently between my finger and thumb and willed them to disappear. I had concluded the previous day in my room that my ability to make other things invisible seemed to be linked to their size or weight, and this theory was borne out as the mints faded away in moments. Taking great care not to make a noise by rattling the box, I slipped them into my pocket. Then I realised I hadn't really thought this through. Mrs Rai was standing just a few feet away from me at the till, with a clear view of the door behind me. There was no way I could open it without her noticing, especially with that bell on the door. After a moment's hesitation, I crept down to the far end of the room where the breakfast cereals were stacked. They looked as good a diversion as any so I singled out a luridly coloured box of Crispy Spews, or something like that, and sent them toppling onto the floor. This triggered a domino effect and the contents of half the shelf ended up in the aisle, making a real racket in the otherwise quiet shop.

Mrs Rai looked up from her paper in surprise, and then hastened over, muttering, "Oh dear, oh dear, an accident," in her quiet voice.

While she was busy picking the boxes up, I rushed back to the door and slipped outside. No doubt Mrs Rai would think it strange to hear the bell ring again without anyone coming in, but it could easily be dismissed as one of life's little mysteries, which would hardly have been the case if she had seen the door open on its own right in front of her.

Walking back towards home, I felt a strong sense of shame and self-loathing. What the hell was I doing stealing from Mr and Mrs Rai? I was in a weird mood because of my frustrations with Lucy, but that was no excuse. "There must be a million and one cool things I could do with my invisibility that wouldn't make me feel disgusted at myself," I thought, stopping in my tracks. "Stealing these mints wasn't just wrong, it also shows a lack of imagination."

These were strong words with which to berate myself, because my imagination is a point of pride for me. I've always pitied people who lack any sort of spark of invention in their nature – and now here I was doing the sort of thing any brain-dead moron might try on finding themselves invisible. I turned and hurried back to the shop, ducking behind a large advertising board just outside to become visible again.

When I walked into the shop Mrs Rai was still behind the till, so I went over to her and began, "I'm so sorry, but I think I forgot to pay for these last time I was in." I showed her the mints, and fished around in my pocket for the money.

"That's OK dear," she replied, with a sad smile, "I understand. You keep them, please."

"No, look, I have the money here," I said, holding it out towards her.

She shook her head. "Please… just a little gift for a good girl."

I kept my hand held out rather awkwardly in front of me for a while, but it was clear she wasn't taking the money so eventually I withdrew it.

"Thanks," I mumbled, and backed out of the little shop, somehow feeling even worse about the whole episode. Once outside, I squeezed behind the advertising board and blinked out again, thinking that I might as well get some more practice on my way home. As I walked back towards our house I went past a couple of people coming in the other direction, and made an effort to tread extra quietly as our paths crossed to make sure they wouldn't be alarmed by my ghostly footsteps. I obviously did a good job on this because they remained lost in their own little worlds and didn't notice me at all, but I made a mental note to go through my shoes and find the quietest pair. That way I could relax a bit more while I was invisible and not be constantly worrying about someone hearing me.

Approaching our next-door neighbour's house I saw their dog, Thornton, basking in the last of the evening sunshine. I slowed down and tried to creep by as silently as I could, but almost immediately he sprang up and rushed over to the fence at the front of his lawn, barking frantically. Then he put his front paws on the fence and started his high-pitched whining, occasionally tailing off into a little howl. This wasn't uncommon; he was a good-natured if slightly imbecilic little beast, and got equally excited every time he met me. I was surprised he'd managed to detect my presence, but of course dogs have their enhanced senses of smell and hearing to help them.

"Shush, shush, good boy, please shush," I implored, reaching out to stroke and soothe him, hoping to calm him down before David, his owner, came out to see what the cause of all the noise was. To my surprise he inclined his head to nuzzle against my approaching hand. Startled, I drew it back, and then slowly extended my arm again. Same result – as soon as my fingers were within a few inches of his little brown snout, he leaned in as if hoping for a scratch around the ears.

"Can you… see me, boy?" I whispered.

"Yep," he replied.

Not really. This isn't that sort of story. But he did look right at me, his tongue lolling out of the side of his mouth and his tail wagging away like he was preparing for take-off. As an experiment, I leaned a little to the left, then a little to the right, and found the dog's big brown eyes following my movements. I crept a little further down the path, and Thornton bounded after me, throwing his paws on the fence again directly in front of me. When I ducked down behind the fence out of his view, he started whining. As soon as I straightened up again, the whining stopped.

"You *can* see me!"

I was about to conduct some more tests when I heard the front door of the house opening and David calling, "Come on Thorny! What's all this whining for?"

Without stopping to worry about my footsteps being heard I turned and fled home as quickly as I could, terrified that silly dog would give me away. Taking cover in our porch, I quickly blinked back in before unlocking the door and running up to my room. Throwing myself on my bed, I went over the last ten minutes in my head while waiting for my heart to stop hammering. I'd learned one thing for sure, I was not cut out to be the world's first super-villain. Not only did I lack the criminal instinct required to steal a tiny pack of mints, I had also stumbled across my kryptonite: slobbering spaniels.

7.

The following morning I woke up early, and used the time writing a detailed account of my experiences with invisibility in my diary. I made it like a science project, noting down the date and time I first disappeared, how long it took the first time I managed to do it on purpose, and how that transition time had rapidly shortened over the following twenty-four hours. I included a section about the dog, and resolved to test my power on other animals when I got an opportunity.

It felt good to get it all down on paper, and by the time I tucked my diary back in its place under my floorboards I felt a lot more cheerful about my situation. Maybe it was for the best I hadn't had a chance to tell Lucy. After all, no matter how good a friend she was, could I really expect anyone to keep a secret this huge? It would be tough for a nun who had taken a vow of silence, let alone the planet's most talkative teenage girl.

By now I felt hungry for some breakfast, so I went downstairs to see what food I could find. My favourite thing to have first thing in the morning was my mum's fresh pancakes with honey and blue-berries, but it seemed like she'd been leaving for work really early lately, so I hadn't had them for weeks. With my new positive frame of mind I de-cided I could make them myself – hey, I'd even make some for Dad, help get him out of his normal morn-ing zombified state.

Annoyingly, the milk was a day or two past its sell-by date, but it smelled okay so I assumed it would be fine. I mixed it together with some flour and eggs and started flipping. There were a few casualties – there always are when I cook anything – but before long I had a stack of four acceptable pancakes ready to go. They were a bit lumpy in places where I hadn't quite mixed the batter well enough, but I didn't think Dad would mind; it's the thought that counts, right? I could hear him bumbling around upstairs so I squirted on some honey and took a couple of the pancakes up for him. He was wandering around looking for socks and looked surprised when I thrust the plate towards him.

"Oh... err... thanks," he mumbled, taking the food and then just standing there holding it like he had no idea what to do with it.

"Gosh, Dad, I know you're not a morning person but come on – you know how to eat pancakes, Mum makes them all the time." I took the fork and loaded it up, then moved it towards his face like he was a baby. "Here comes the train, coming towards the tunnel. Chugga-chugga-chugga, chugga-chugga-chugga – now open up the tunnel for me…"

He batted my hand away and then grabbed the fork saying, "Sorry, Maddie, I do appreciate it. I know you're doing your best. I'll have these in a minute."

He wandered off to continue his search for socks while I got ready for school. It was Friday, the best day of the school week, and as I dressed I felt determined to make it just a normal day and not think too much about invisibility. I didn't need to answer those big questions about who I should tell and what I should do with my power right away, and I was determined to get back to just enjoying life like I used to. I cast my mind back a month or so to when Lucy and I had gone to the ice skating rink. We were completely hopeless and clung to the sides like barnacles, but we'd had such a good time my face hurt from smiling too much by the end of it. My backside hurt too actually, thanks to a couple of slips, but it was all part of the fun. So, that's what I was going to get back to – just fun, fun, fun and not worrying about anything related to my superpower.

As we were leaving the house for school I found that Dad hadn't actually eaten his pancakes, which was aggravating, but in my cheerful frame of mind I was able to overlook it. I'd eaten mine and I have to say they were excellent, so his loss! Arriving at school I saw Lucy, Sophia and the others chattering away in our usual corner while awaiting the bell. Today I felt no burning urge to get Lucy on her own to share my news, so I just quietly joined the group, ready to discuss more mundane subjects.

Unfortunately, Lucy wasn't on the same page, and greeted me with a loud fanfare before beating her hands on Sophia's backpack to achieve a drum-roll effect. "Ladies and gentlemen, step right up and buy your tickets please! The Lucy Wolfe Circus is proud to present the one, the only – the amazing Maddie Sykes!" she hollered, in what I assume was intended to be a cockney accent. Then she started capering around me, advertising my biggest ever secret to anyone who would listen. "Now you see her, now you don't… where does she go? Nobody knows, no-one can ever understand the dark secrets behind the sinister illusions of the incredible invisible girl!"

I froze in absolute horror for a moment. It seemed like my worst fear was coming to life in front of me – my invisibility revealed to the whole world. I needn't have worried though: after a second or two of surprised silence, most of the others began laughing at Lucy's ridiculous antics.

"What are you going on about, you utter spamhead?" asked Sophia, putting her arm around my shoulders protectively, but giggling nonetheless.

"What's so amazing about Maddie? No offence, Maddie."

Lucy calmed down a little and explained, "So Maddie tried to fool me with this bizarre 'Hey look, I can disappear' thing last night when we were on a chat, she was all, 'You can't see me, ooooh, spooky! Beware my dark magic, I'm coming to get you, and I'll haunt you for a thousand years, and steal your rabbit, and stuff,' and I was like, 'No way,' but she was like, 'Yuh-huh!' – crazy, right?"

I had to smile at Lucy's typically inaccurate memory of our conversation, which for some reason she maintained the cockney accent while sharing. Sophia and the rest of the group turned to me for an explanation, so I just said I'd been messing about with a new filter on my phone, and then swiftly turned the conversation towards other matters. The topic was soon forgotten with no real harm done, although Lucy insisted on calling me "The Amazing Maddie Sykes" for the rest of the morning.

After lunch we had English Literature as our first class. We'd been studying Hamlet, which was okay although not exactly what I'd call the greatest play ever written. Our teacher, Miss Dawkins, started by handing back some tests from the previous week. I couldn't actually even remember doing this test, and I was a little surprised to see my answer to the first question. It was a nice easy one: *Is Hamlet indecisive? Ensure your answer illustrates your thinking.* Bizarrely, I had answered this by drawing a picture of myself, with a thought bubble coming out of my head like in a comic, simply containing the word "Yes".

Flipping through the pages I found that I had basically phoned in the whole thing, with not one single sensible or worthwhile answer to be seen. I nervously turned to the last page to see Miss Dawkins' comments and the inevitable "F" grade, fearing there might be an instruction to take this paper to the headmistress's office and explain it to her.

I was in for another surprise – there was no grade at all, and rather than tearing into me or sending me to the head she had simply written, "Let's have a little chat about this."

A little chat? Miss Dawkins was a frosty old lady of at least forty, and was not what you could call "chatty" by any stretch of the imagination. In the past she'd given me a real roasting for missing out an apostrophe, so I didn't imagine the chat she had in mind would be a pleasant one. I sighed; she was probably going to make me stay behind at the end of the lesson.

Miss Dawkins sat down behind her desk and read us the last scene from the play, then began asking questions about it.

"To what extent was Hamlet responsible for his mother's death?"

This was my chance to redeem myself and win some goodwill ahead of the dreaded "chat". Despite my stupid answers in the test, I actually knew the play pretty well and felt I could easily spend a couple of minutes giving a praiseworthy answer on that topic. I threw my hand up, putting on exactly the expression of eager enthusiasm for learning you would expect from a person who was essentially a model student and just happened to have messed up one or two little exam questions. Nobody else seemed keen to pitch in on the subject, the rest of the class keeping their hands rooted to their desks. Weirdly though, Miss Dawkins didn't turn straight to me, and continued to scan the room as if waiting for somebody else to raise their hand. My desk for this lesson was right on the back row, so I waved my arm around just in case she hadn't seen me. To my annoyance, Miss Dawkins swept her gaze right over me without asking for my answer. Was she angry about how badly I'd done in the test? I guessed this must be the reason she was ignoring me, and that just made me more annoyed. This was one of my best subjects – unlike a lot of people in my year I actually enjoyed reading, and sometimes we studied books in class that I'd already read just for fun, like Animal Farm. Not that it's exactly a fun read, in fact it made me cry, but you know what I mean. The point is, I knew I contributed more to that class than anyone else, so it hurt to be suddenly ignored just because I'd written a few jokey answers.

What happened next just wasn't like me at all, but in my defence one of my absolute pet hates is when people ignore me. Plus, like I said, I'd been a bit down for the past couple of weeks for whatever reason, and then there was all this stuff with the invisibility going on – basically, there were extenuating circumstances. As my irritation with Miss Dawkins mounted, I found myself scrunching the failed test into a ball and then hurling it in the teacher's direction as hard as I could. "Try ignoring that!" I thought bitterly, as the balled-up paper arrowed towards her, before a thought struck me.

What if she wasn't ignoring me? What if...? I glanced down, and found to my dismay that sure enough, it had happened again. There was nothing to be seen but an empty seat where my body should have been. I looked up again just in time to see my throw find its target, the ball of paper pinging off the side of Miss Dawkins' head as she stood looking at the desks over by the window.

There was a hushed silence, then the sound of thirty chairs scraping as everyone turned to see where the throw had come from. Of course, they didn't see anyone in my seat, so people's eyes turned enquiringly to the other children sitting near me. Meanwhile, Miss Dawkins stooped to pick up the paper and unfolded it on her desk. I held my breath, cursing the moment of madness that had made me throw something with my own name written on the front of it. The teacher slowly smoothed out the sheets of paper, and then turned to look towards my desk.

This was a nightmare – she would probably come and look around at the back of the class, expecting me to be hiding. The other kids might join in, and someone would be sure to bump into me in my invisible state, freaking themselves out and exposing my secret. I had to get out of there. If she couldn't find me, Miss Dawkins would have to conclude that I must have slipped out of the room while she was reading, and that someone else had thrown my test at her. I slipped out of my chair as quietly as I could, and began to stealthily creep up the aisle between the desks, on tiptoes to make as little sound as possible. It seemed to be going well until I reach the front of the class and heard first a snort, and then an explosion of suppressed laughter from behind me.

Whirling around, I saw that it came from Liza Preston – my nemesis – who was now pointing right at me and howling with spiteful laughter. There was an echo of more muted sniggering from the rest of the class, and I found that every single person in the room had their eyes fixed on me. I barely needed to glance down at my hands to confirm that I had reappeared at some point, and they had all watched me sneaking towards the front of the room like an excessively nervous ninja on their first day at ninja school.

What the hell? This was getting ridiculous, how was I going to explain my behaviour now? "Errr, just need to, um… you know… go out there for a second," I mumbled, dashing past Miss Dawkins and out into the hallway. I took a left and ran all the way to the girls' changing room, where I locked myself into one of the toilet cubicles and sat for a few minutes with my head in my hands.

"I wish I'd never discovered this stupid invisibility – it's not even a proper superpower, it's more like a super liability! Why can't everything just go back to how it was?"

As I often found, after spending a little while cursing the cruel world that was constantly against me and concluding that I was the unluckiest person on the whole planet, a bit of perspective and common sense started to kick in. I couldn't completely blame my unreliable invisibility for what just happened – it wouldn't have been a problem if I hadn't gone into a strop and stupidly thrown that paper at Miss Dawkins. I really didn't have any more reason to complain than a kid who gets given the world's coolest bike and then falls off it while trying to do a wheelie. I just needed to concentrate more to make sure I stayed hidden, and it was starting to look like maybe I needed to concentrate on staying visible sometimes too! This sounded like a horrible burden, having to keep that in my mind at all times, but perhaps it would get easier. Over time I imagined it might become something I would do subconsciously, like breathing or being awesome. I smiled at that last thought, and started to cheer up, but my thoughts turned to the rest of my class. Had they seen me reappear? I concluded they couldn't have done, or there would have been gasps of shock rather than laughter.

"I bet I faded back in when they all looked over to see what Miss Dawkins was going to do with the paper ball," I speculated. "So I guess they saw me get up from my chair and creep the whole length of the classroom, like a certifiable weirdo. It must have seemed odd I wasn't at my desk a second before, but I suppose they must have thought I'd hidden under it, or something."

Something didn't seem quite right about that picture, but it was the only logical way I could explain the reaction of the other kids. I resolved to try and find out from Lucy what she had seen, and rose from the seat to go back into class and face the music. Stepping back inside the room, I stood by the door wearing my meekest and most apologetic expression, unsure of whether to say anything to explain my behaviour. Luckily, Miss Dawkins was in the middle of a long, droning monologue about Polonius, and simply waved me to my seat rather than stopping to chastise me. I hurried to the back of the room with my head down, trying to ignore the stares of the other students. Their expressions ranged from sympathy (Lucy and Sophia) through idle curiosity of the sort one might feel at the zoo when looking at a baboon (most of the class) all the way down to malicious glee (Liza).

At the end of the lesson I tried to keep my head down and slip away unnoticed, but I knew I wasn't likely to get off that lightly.

"Madeline – a word please," the teacher called, just as I was getting within range of the exit. She stood waiting for the others to leave and then gestured towards a chair, close to her desk. I went and sat down, bracing myself for a roasting. I always find it's best to speak first in these situations, so I dived in just as she was about to begin.

"I'm really sorry... not sure what happened... you know I'm not normally like that," I babbled, waiting for a plausible explanation to pop into my head. "It's just... erm... you know how sometimes you can just... and then... you know?" I wasn't making any sense. I needed to up my game here. Then it hit me.

"Girl problems!" I blurted. "Yeah, just really suffering with – you know – girl problems. Girl issues. Female challenges. Womanly woes. You know what I mean?"

Lucy had told me she'd had a lot of success with this tactic when she got into trouble with Mr Bates, our science teacher, a few weeks earlier. Difference was, he was a man – men don't like talking about that sort of thing, do they? On reflection, I doubted it was going to phase Miss Dawkins, but I waited in hope for her response. I like to set myself realistic, attainable goals; right now, my goal was just to get out of this conversation without being sent to see the headmistress.

Miss Dawkins gave me a sad smile and said nothing for a moment. Had I touched on a sensitive area? Like I said, she was pretty ancient – perhaps she no longer had to worry about "girl problems", and would find the mention of the subject painful. However, when she spoke it was in surprisingly sympathetic tones.

"Madeline, I know that sometimes things can get on top of us and we can feel like we're in a dark place. I want you to know that the best way to deal with this kind of, erm, problem, is often just to talk about it. So, if you want to talk, then please feel as though you can come to me."

This was great – it looked like I'd played it perfectly! If anything, she'd gone for my lame excuse even more readily than Mr Bates had with Lucy. I reminded myself to thank my friend for her wise advice when I got out of here. I just had to wrap things up carefully.

"Yeah, OK, thanks," I mumbled, forcing myself to make eye contact for that extra touch of sincerity. "I appreciate that."

Miss Dawkins eyes darted away uncomfortably in return, but she pressed on. "So is there anything you would like to discuss right now?"

"Erm, no, I don't think so, not right this moment, but if there is something... you know, in the future... then of course..." I trailed off, leaving the possibility of talking in the future hanging there without actually committing to anything. Standing up, I edged towards the door.

"You're a good student, Madeline, with a bright future ahead of you. Just remember that, please."

"Yes... I will... thank you..."

With those words, I was out of the door and hurrying away down the corridor. Mission accomplished! I hadn't been sent to see the head, and my parents hadn't been called, so overall it was a great result. That said, there were reasons I couldn't feel completely happy. Why the hell had I lost it like that and thrown my test at Miss Dawkins? It was so unlike me to lose my temper, and I vowed to keep myself under better control from now on. Calm, logical and laid-back, that was me; there was no reason anything should change just because I had a kick-ass superpower. Did I though? That was my other concern; I needed to properly master my invisibility so I could make it the huge advantage and source of enjoyment it should be, rather than a worry and – based on my experience in the classroom back there – an embarrassment.

8.

We had a short break before our next lesson, so most of my year group were lounging around outside. A few of the boys were playing football, while a slightly larger number looked like they were having a contest to see who could spit phlegm the farthest, organised by that weasel Leon. Why can't boys act like civilised human beings and spend their free time talking? Surely there are only so many times you can enjoy kicking, throwing or indeed spitting on things before it loses its appeal.

I turned my attention to the girls. Sure enough, most of them were clustered in small groups, deep in conversation. The only exception was Jess, who was climbing a tree over by the fence – the tree we had been forbidden to climb ever since a boy in the year above ours fell out of it and fractured his face, or something. If I turned invisible I could climb that tree as often as I liked, but unlike Jess I didn't get a lot of enjoyment from doing things like that on my own. Once again, I found myself wishing that Lucy could share my power and I scanned the swarm of faces, looking for her. I soon located her over by the unused basketball hoop, with Sophia and a couple of the other girls. Were they talking about me? Probably. I'd made such and idiot of myself in class, it was inevitable I'd be the subject of some ridicule for the rest of the day – maybe for the rest of my life. No, I told myself, no need to be melodramatic: things like this get talked about for an hour or two and then the focus moves

98

on to something new, like last week when that video of a bucket full of baby sloths was going around.

It would be interesting to know what they were saying though, wouldn't it? I looked at Lucy's group again. Little Olivia was there, her green eyes sparkling with laughter as she talked, while the more timid Rosie stood just behind her, listening to the others with that shy half-smile of hers. Sophia stood with her arm around Lucy, nodding in agreement with whatever Olivia was saying and sharing in the joke. Was the laughter at my expense? You always like to imagine your best friend will have your back no matter what, but what would Lucy do if the others were being mean about me? Sophia, Olivia and Rosie were kind of our friends too, but not like Lucy and me – more like the kind of friends you talk to when your real friend isn't around. Did Lucy feel like that though? Perhaps she liked them as much as she liked me. Maybe if they made jokes about me, she would join in.

"Don't be so stupid," I told myself. "We're best friends. Best. Bar none. We've had all the best friend talks, and shared the best friend secrets – like which boys we like, and which boys we hate (mostly the latter), and what we'll call our kids if we have any, and where we would bury the body if we murdered someone. If I can't rely on her, I can't rely on anyone in this horrible world."

Still, there she was, yakking away with the others – she had to be saying something about me, and I felt an overpowering urge to find out what.

"This will be good practice," I told myself, by way of justifying my actions. "It's not just about spying on my friends – this is about gaining better control of my power."

Stepping back inside the school doors, I glanced behind me to check the corridor was deserted, then quickly blinked out. I waved my hands around in front of my face, just in case, and was pleased to find I'd achieved complete invisibility in no more than a second.

"Let's just make sure I maintain it this time," I told myself sternly. I needed to focus to avoid a repeat of the fiasco from earlier, so I slowly edged back outside while retaining a clear image of my invisible self in my mind. It's surprisingly difficult to picture something being invisible, but I did it by imagining a view of my surroundings seen from a distance – a view without me in it – and this seemed to work.

Once outside, I took another look around. The door into the school was at the top of a short flight of steps, giving me a perfect vantage point from which to plan my next move. Lucy was still over by the hoop, but just below me on the other side of the low wall that ran alongside the steps I saw that Leon and one of his friends had left the spitting contest and were having what looked like a very secretive little chat. Were they talking about me? Only one way to find out – I stooped to keep the wall between me and them, and crept down a couple of steps so I could listen in.

At first I couldn't make out what they were saying over the babble of noise from the other kids, but after a moment I was able to tune into their whispers.

"… and tell Brooksy, yeah, he better not get the same trainers as me or I'll cut him, yeah? And tell him he needs to, like, stay away from Jade, 'coz she's mine yeah? Tell him I know people – everyone knows I know people – but tell him anyway, yeah? Not just people, obviously – bad people. People who can mess him up. Not that I need people to mess him up. Because *I* can mess him up, yeah?"

The recipient of this nonsense was a member of Leon's entourage, Kyle. Although less annoying than his friend, Kyle was not the sharpest pencil in the case, and replied, "OK, yeah, I hear ya – so you want Brooksy to stay away from Jade's trainers, or you'll hurt him, right? Or someone else will, or whatever."

"No!" hissed Leon, irritably. "You're not listening. Let's keep this simple. Just tell him, yeah, to keep away from me, my trainers, and my girl… or somebody's gonna get hurt."

"Right, yeah. And I'm guessing that 'somebody' is…"

"Yes, him, obviously! You feel me?"

"I feel you, yeah. Feelin' you, defo. Wait, do you want me to feel you?"

I suppressed a giggle that would have given me away. Leon loved to imagine himself as a kid from the mean streets, living life on the edge, with notorious crack dealers for parents and dangerous criminals for friends. In fact, nothing could be further from the truth – he lived in a nice big house in the suburbs and his dad was an accountant, while his mum volunteered at the library and was best known for her badminton skills.

Still, the main thing was, they weren't talking about me. It was time to find out if the same could be said of my friends. My invisibility was holding up well, but I still felt a bit insecure after the problems earlier so I took an indirect route around the edge of the playground, thinking that if I did suddenly reappear it would be best if I was standing somewhere nobody would notice. On my way towards Lucy and the others I went past a couple more girls from our class, Ellen and Amy. They were sitting on the floor with their backs to me, and I couldn't resist creeping a little closer to find out what they were talking about.

"... thinks she's so special, it makes me sick!" I heard Amy exclaim with considerable venom.

"Totally know what you mean," Ellen agreed, "and the worst thing is, there's absolutely nothing special about her."

God, were they talking about me? I didn't really know them that well, but we'd always got on okay. Did they think I was attention seeking in class, and now they hated me?

"Plus, I've actually scored more goals than her this season, even though she's been playing in my position," Amy continued.

Panic over. They were both on the hockey team, so they were obviously unhappy with one of the other players. It could possibly have been Sophia actually, as she had recently joined the squad, but the key thing was that it obviously wasn't me: I'd played hockey maybe three times in my life and acquired the nickname "little tiny goalie" because they always put me in goal, where a person of my small stature was unlikely to thrive.

I moved on, and paused when I got within earshot of my friends, maybe five yards from their group. More conscious than ever of the awkwardness reappearing would cause, I lurked behind a big recycling bin and strained my ears. The first voice I heard was Olivia's.

"I still just can't believe she did that. I mean, it was so funny, but it's not exactly Maddie is it?"

How rude! I was funny, wasn't I? What was she saying, that it was surprising to be entertained by me, because usually being with me was like watching paint dry?

To my relief Lucy dived in. "Well, actually Maddie is really funny, in fact she regularly leaves me in need of medical attention because I've ruptured six organs laughing at her."

"No, no, I'm not saying she's not funny, she's very, erm, well, she's very sarcastic isn't she? Insult humour, smack talk, great – Maddie's your girl – but throwing stuff at the teacher and then prancing around the classroom like a lunatic? If anything I'd say that's more your style, Luce…"

Lucy slapped her arm in good natured indignation, and replied, "I just hope she doesn't get in too much trouble."

"Under the circumstances, I think she'll be fine," Sophia assured her. "Did anyone see *Love Asylum* last night? It was so sweet the way George wanted to run after Ashleigh but he couldn't tie his shoelaces."

With that, they were on to a heated discussion about the contestants on a stupid reality show I hadn't seen. I waited a while to see if they would talk about me again but they didn't, and I found myself weirdly disappointed. I remembered something my dad said to me years ago, "You wouldn't worry about what other people thought of you if you knew how seldom they did".

I was about to slink away, planning to go inside and blink back in once I got to the girls bathroom just to be safe, when I heard an unpleasantly whiny voice that I knew only too well.

"Hey Lucy, where's your crazy little friend? Sent to see Miss Parker? Or has she been taken straight to the young offenders' centre where she belongs? I know she's been desperate for people to look at her ever since she lost all the weight, but that was pathetic even by her low standards."

The voice belonged to the loathsome Liza Preston, who had approached the little group of girls and was standing just on the other side of the bin, no more than a couple of feet away from me. Had I lost weight? Not to my knowledge, but who knew what went on in Liza's vengeful imagination.

"Get lost, Liza," Lucy replied, her voice dripping with contempt. "What Maddie did was the funniest thing that's happened in class for weeks, and as usual you're jealous."

"She's not funny, she's mad! She needs locking up," Liza spat back, although she also took a step backwards, perhaps fearing how Lucy might respond. This put her even closer to me, and I found myself presented with the opportunity to do exactly what Lucy had jokingly suggested I should do with my power – namely, to give Liza a swift kick up the backside. Even with her back to me, I felt like I could see the self-satisfied smirk on her face as she congratulated herself on not letting a day go by without insulting me in some way. Images rushed through my mind of my worst moments at school, like the time I got that really bad haircut or the time I was cast as one of the ugly sisters in Cinderella and had to pretend to be in love with Leon, who had been chosen as Prince Charming in a rare display of irony from our Drama teacher. At each of these harrowing times in my life, and many more, there was Liza: pointing, laughing, and making vicious little comments to her cackling coven of followers.

This was my chance to get even. My right foot positively itched to travel the short distance between us at speed and deal out some retribution, and I prepared myself, planning a route by which to slip away once the deed was done. At the last moment though, I stopped myself. Lucy and I prided ourselves on the cold, don't-mess-with-us personas we often adopted at school – in fact we used to call ourselves "The Psychotic Sisterhood" – but this was really just an act, an unemotional veneer to help protect against people like Liza. Underneath it I loved kittens and puppies, helped old ladies if they dropped their shopping, and I had never kicked a person in anger in my whole life. Something I couldn't quite put my finger on told me this wasn't the time to change all that. I'd settle things with Liza someday, and wipe that smile off her poisonous lips, but I'd do it in the open, face to face – not by sneaking around like an invisible coward.

In another moment, the opportunity was gone. Lucy had opted to ignore Liza's last comment, and had dropped her voice so my nemesis couldn't hear what she was saying to the others. Sensing there was no more mileage to be had from further taunts at this point, Liza turned and marched away to where some of her lackeys were gathered.

By now it was nearly time for our last class of the day, so I left my spot behind the bin and headed back towards the school doors. I started off by carefully making my way along the outskirts of the playground, as I had done on my way over to the basketball hoop, but my invisibility was holding up so well that I got a bit blasé and decided to take a shortcut through a more crowded area to save time. It wasn't the best decision I'd made on that difficult day: some boys in the year above had convinced themselves they were future NFL stars and had picked the patch I was crossing as their end zone. I heard footsteps running towards me and turned just in time to see an airborne ball and two sprinting players descending on the exact point I was standing. There was no time to get out of the way, or do anything more than put my arms up to cover my face before both boys collided with me and all three of us hit the deck, hard.

Searing pain shot through my body, and the world span around before my eyes for a few seconds as I lay on my back, unable to breathe.

"Where the hell did she come from?" I heard one of the boys grunt, as they picked themselves up.

I closed my eyes for a few moments, trying to get my breath back. The pain, which had initially seemed to come from every inch of my body, resolved itself into a dull ache in my ribs, plus a sharp pain in my elbow from where I'd hit the ground. It was bad, but manageable – I wasn't going to cry. I never cry. Well, almost never.

Eventually my breathing came back and I opened my eyes to find a hand hovering in front of me. The hand belonged to Jake, who was leaning over me with a look of concern.

"Are you okay?" he asked. "Really sorry, I just didn't see you there when I threw that pass. You must have taken quite a hit from these lumps." He gestured towards my two accidental assailants who were standing nearby looking suitably sheepish, although one of them mumbled some rubbish about "girls needing to understand the dangers of the end zone".

I grabbed his hand and got carefully to my feet, checking myself for injuries and also making sure I'd become fully visible again at the moment of impact.

"I'm fine," I replied after a moment or two. "No big deal."

As it was Jake, and he'd apologised, I didn't want to make a fuss about it – especially under the circumstances.

"Are you sure you're okay? Your elbow is bleeding."

He was still holding on to my hand, and looked genuinely remorseful about my scrapes and bruises, not knowing that it really wasn't his fault and there was no way he could have seen me.

"It's nothing, really," I insisted. This statement was blatantly untrue, as I literally had blood dripping from my elbow and forming a little puddle on the ground at my feet, but like I said, I didn't want to make it a big thing and attract even more attention. Really, I needed to go and get my arm looked at, or at least find a bandage of some sort, but just for a second it felt nice to have someone acting so concerned about my wellbeing. Inevitably, that warm feeling was ruined a second later by the sound of my least favourite voice in the whole wide world.

"Wow, Maddie, I knew you were desperate for a boyfriend but seriously – now you're literally throwing yourself at boys? Two of them at once... just when I thought you couldn't sink any lower!"

I didn't need to turn around to know that these words came from the malicious tongue of Liza Preston, who rushed over with a couple of her sidekicks saying, "Just ignore her Jake, she'd do anything to get your attention."

I snatched my hand away from Jake and took off, up the steps and back inside the school, unable to make out the content of Jake's response to Liza in my haste. Why did life always conspire to put her within six feet of me every time anything bad happened? As I made my way towards the school office in search of the first aid kit, I reflected bitterly that comic book superheroes had proper, impressive archenemies with names like "Dr Death" or "Megakill", and what did I have? "Snarkface Girl" – destroying the world one nasty comment at a time.

9.

Mum and Dad weren't around when I got home that night, so I decided to bring my diary downstairs and work on it in the living room. I took advantage of the rare opportunity to sit in Mum's chair, which was by far the most comfortable. It was also the best situated, holding the prime position closest to the TV. I sat cross-legged on the squashy brown leather and recorded the day's events, treating it like a proper scientific journal. There were some positives to report, such as the length of time I'd been able to stay invisible when I was out in the playground, and how quickly I'd been able to blink in and out. On a less positive note, there was my loss of concentration and reappearance in the classroom, plus my erratic behaviour in throwing my test at Miss Dawkins. Could that have been linked to my power in some way? Perhaps the changes in me went beyond my new ability, and I was changing into a different person. I parked that scary thought and wondered again about sharing my secret with my parents. I pictured a rosy scene where they were happy and excited for me, but also very supportive – calmly discussing the best ways to use my power while still leading a normal life. Maybe with their help and advice I really could become a superhero like in the comics, and save the world, or the whale, or something. Eventually I'd receive a knighthood from the queen, and fifty foot high statues would be built to celebrate my deeds – and at every step, my parents would be there to guide me, support me, and cheer me on.

I let myself dwell on that warm and cosy fantasy for a while, before eventually dismissing it with a rueful shake of my head. Mum was a worrier, and her first thought would be that turning invisible might be bad for my health. She would want me to be tested – exactly what I wanted to avoid. Dad would disagree, and there would be a fight between them with me in the middle, as usual. No, I concluded, I wouldn't be telling them. If anything I was even surer that I'd made the right decision in keeping my secret to myself.

I went up to my room and put the diary away in its hiding place, then went to the mirror to look at my injuries from earlier. To my surprise, when I looked at my face I saw redness around my eyes and moisture on my cheeks. I gently touched the liquid with my finger and gave it an experimental lick. Salty. What the hell? It was like I'd been crying, but I never cry! I was hardly likely to do it without even noticing. I peered at my tear-stained face again. I looked tired, really tired. Worn out. Maybe that was the main issue here: this invisibility stuff was a lot to take on board. It was quite understandable that I wasn't going to be sleeping well, and my mental state would suffer as a result. As soon as I got more used to it, I'd be back to normal. Either that, or I was turning into some sort of weirdo who caused trouble at school and then came home and cried about it without even realising.

I slept fitfully that night, my dreams haunted by a strange feeling that I was in darkness, and there was something terrible out there, something close by but just out of sight. Each time I woke up I found my pillow uncomfortably wet. "Great, so you're crying in your sleep now," I chastised myself. "There's really nothing to be upset about here: you've got an amazing power, and your ability to control it is getting better and better. You only have to use it when you want to. And as for all this weird behaviour – that's just because you're so tired. There's no need to cry – you're not some prissy princess who turns on the waterworks every time life gets a bit bumpy. Just relax, imagine you're drifting around in an ocean of sleepy calmness, with waves of soothing tiredness washing over you, and you're being carried gently along towards to the dreamy shores of restful sleep… oh yeah, AND STOP CRYING!!!!!"

This seemed to do the trick.

When I next opened my eyes it was morning. Birds sang in the trees outside my window and bright sunlight streamed in through my blinds. To be honest the birds weren't the most talented of vocalists, given that they only knew one song and that song only had one note, but I gave them an A for effort and took the overall effect as a good omen for the day ahead.

Grabbing my phone I noticed it was after 11am. Great! I had obviously needed a really good lie in, and I'd got one. Mum had a habit of getting me up at a ridiculously early hour at the weekend, like 10 o'clock, but perhaps she had realised I needed the rest. My general feeling of well-being took a bit of a hit when I saw I had a message from Lucy cancelling the shopping trip we had planned for that afternoon – her parents had decided to go to their caravan for a couple of days and of course she had to go with them. Still, in my positive frame of mind I didn't let that get me down. She suggested an even better shopping session the following week-end with Olivia, Sophia and some of the other girls, so that was fine.

I read a chapter of my book, then rolled out of bed and pulled some clothes on, really just the first things that came to hand. I decided I might just go and have a wander round the shops on my own, maybe take my book, grab an ice cream in Swirls and just read for a bit. People reading in cafés, or indeed ice cream places, always have an intense and interesting look about them don't they?

I didn't really feel like having breakfast, so I just threw my copy of Wuthering Heights in my backpack and headed out. It's only a ten minute walk from our house to the town centre, and although I normally try to get a lift whenever possible, today I took some pleasure from making the short journey on my own.

It was a nice warm day, and the large park I had to cross on my route was full of people, dogs, and squirrels. I noticed how these last two groups were locked in an eternal cycle of conflict: the squirrels nonchalantly going about their business but always watchful over the approach of their enemies, the dogs. The dogs, in turn, were straining at their leads, longing for a chance to pursue the squirrels. Sometimes, a dog would achieve its dream by slipping its lead or yanking free from its owner, and the

chase would begin. It never lasted long though –
somehow the squirrels had an incredibly accurate
system for triangulating the positions of themselves,
the dogs, and the nearest tree, always ensuring they
could reach safety a split second before they were
caught. Moving to a branch perhaps ten feet from
the ground, they would then regard the disappointed dog with a look of mingled contempt and
smugness, but I felt I also detected a trace of pity.
Did squirrels have the capacity to pity their beaten
opponent? On some level did they empathise with
the resigned droop of the dog's ears as it gave up on
its short vigil at the base of the tree and returned to
its human? Then again, maybe I was reading this all
wrong – maybe the pursuit was its own reward, and
the dogs were in fact leaving the scene with the quiet
satisfaction of a job well done, thinking "Dogs 1,
Squirrels 0". Perhaps because I was in a positive
frame of mind, I concluded as I left the park that the
two sides had a mutually beneficial relationship

from which they both got some pleasure – the dogs loved vanquishing the intruders from their ground-level domain, while the squirrels enjoyed having the last laugh, resuming their squirrelly activities on the grass mere moments after the dogs were led away.

On this happy thought, I joined the crowd of people milling around the shops and restaurants of the town centre. Directing my steps towards the in-door shopping area that housed most of the best clothes shops, I browsed through the sale racks at a few of my favourite places. It wasn't quite the same without Lucy there, making me try on ridiculously garish clothes and joining in with my sarcastic comments about the other shoppers, but I found that my light-hearted mood persisted anyway.

In the second shop I visited, I found a couple of really nice hoodies. One was red, my favourite colour, with "Brooklyn 1905" written across the front in white letters. The second one was grey, but with sparkly lettering spelling out "Amour Perdu".

Everyone knows "Amour" means "Love" in French, but I wasn't so sure about "Perdu" – a quick check on my phone revealed it means "Lost", so presumably "Lost Love". I'd never been in love, so it wasn't especially relevant, but there was still something about it I really liked. Possibly the font. I wanted them both, but had very little cash on me, only enough for one of them, so I tried to make a decision. Lucy would have advised the red one because she hates sparkly things – she wouldn't like that jazzy French text. My dad, on the other hand, would love the grey one because of the educational benefit of wearing some French vocab, while pouring scorn on the red one.

"There's nothing special about Brooklyn," he would say, "it's just a boring suburb of New York. You might as well wear a hoodie that says 'Croydon 1905'."

Then again, he knows nothing about fashion, and in fact it wasn't down to either of them – it was my choice. Problem was, I couldn't decide. I hated the thought of putting either of them back for someone else to pick up, but I had to do it. Or did I? I glanced around furtively. I could see a couple of cameras, plus a few members of staff busy with other customers. What if I turned invisible and just slipped out of here? It was a fairly cheap shop, and they didn't put security tags on their clothes, so no worries there. I stepped behind a rack of bulky coats which screened me from both the cameras and the staff, and quickly blinked out. To my dismay I found that the two hoodies stayed in view, hanging weirdly in mid-air under my invisible arm. It had been a while since I tried to make something else disappear, and I'd actually forgotten it wouldn't just happen automatically.

I recalled how I'd failed to make my furniture and school bag disappear, and had concluded that heavier things were more difficult. So, this was going to be a test of how my powers had developed:

the combined weight of the hoodies felt a fair bit more than my bag. I closed my eyes and focused hard on imagining the clothes fading away, taking it nice and slowly and allowing at least ten seconds before I took a peek. Success! They had vanished so perfectly I had to give them a squeeze just to make sure they were still there. I then advanced towards the entrance of the shop. It didn't have a doorway as such, just a wide opening out into the shopping centre. I paused a couple of steps away from the change of flooring tiles which marked the edge of the shop's territory. Did I really want to do this? It wasn't like taking something from Mrs Rai's shop, because this was no family-run business, just a faceless multinational corporation who paid pitiful wages for their clothes to be made by three-year-olds in Asia and then sold them in Europe and America for big profits. By taking away some of their ill-gotten gains, wouldn't I be striking a blow for children everywhere? Like a modern-day Robin Hood, almost? I found myself chuckling at the weakness of my own argument. It's not as if I was planning on donating the money I saved by stealing these things to feed under-privileged sweatshop workers. Plus, I imagined that when Faceless Corp lost money to theft they would just use it as an excuse to pay the people in their horrible factories even less.

I was on the point of turning around and putting the hoodies back when a woman wearing an excessive amount of makeup made the decision for me.

"Can I help you with anything at all today?"

I span around in shock and found a shop assistant standing right next to me. I'd obviously been thinking too hard about my ethical dilemma and lost focus on staying invisible.

"No… I'm fine… just looking for my uncle," I blurted. "He's called Bernard." For some reason lost in the mists of time I often involved a fictitious

Uncle Bernard when I had to come up with a lie quickly.

The shop assistant raised a sceptical eyebrow, but had clearly reached the limits of her interest in me and walked away after saying, "Well, just let me know if you need anything at all today," making me wonder if she added a superfluous "at all today" to the end of every sentence. I pictured her having a romantic walk in the moonlight with her lover, and whispering, "Do my eyes melt your heart with the flame of a thousand love candles at all today?"

I headed back into the store and hid the grey hoodie under a pile of ugly pink t shirts bearing the slightly bizarre message "Dreamin' of Cleveland", hoping it would be quite a while before anyone found it and I might still be able to buy it next time I visited. Taking the red one to the till and paying for it, I found myself still feeling quite upbeat. It was no great surprise I'd faded back in just now, as I was thinking too hard about other things. This was just a lesson I was going to have to learn for the future. And as for my indecisiveness over whether to take the clothes, well, looking at this alongside the big moment where I passed up my chance to kick Liza in her richly deserving backside, I guess I'd established once and for all that I would only be using my power for good.

10.

I headed to the bathrooms inside the shopping centre and went into a cubicle, then removed the labels from my purchase and put it on over my t-shirt. The crowds of shoppers presented a great opportunity to work on my skills, and I decided to see if I could do a complete circuit of the centre while maintaining my invisibility. I quickly blinked out, then let the door to my cubicle swing wide open.

Immediately, I realised I'd made a mistake. A large middle-aged woman with ginger hair was heading straight for me, and in the confined space I didn't have room to get past her before she reached the open doorway. Thinking fast, I dropped onto my stomach and crawled under the partition and into the next cubicle, which luckily was empty. Despite my best efforts, the ginger lady's foot bumped against my arm as I pushed myself through, and I heard her exclaim, "What the hell…?"

I lay on the floor for a second until my heart stopped trying to hammer its way out of my chest. That was a close one. Why didn't I just close the door again, and lock it? That would have made a lot more sense. The lady might have thought it was a bit weird, but certainly less weird than stepping on my invisible arm. I guess it's easy to pick the wrong option when you only have a second to think about it. Then something more important occurred to me: I was lying face down in a public toilet. My stomach lurched at the thought of the various unpleasant things this floor might have been in contact with, and I quickly scrambled to my feet. Learning my lesson from a few moments before, I peered out through the crack between the cubicle door and the wall, checked there was nobody nearby, and then fled from the bathrooms as quickly as I could, wishing I could outrun the memory of how bad that floor had smelled.

Back out in the shopping area, I took a moment to calm down. A full-body cringe swept over me, starting at my feet and working its way right up to the roots of my hair, as I struggled to block out all the negative thoughts arising from my latest misadventure. I tried to focus on a more positive note – throughout those unfortunate events I had managed to stay invisible, and looking down at where my legs should have been I could safely say that I'd never been more transparent. It was time to carry on with my plan and do a full tour of the shopping centre without anyone seeing me.

I started off confidently, keeping my mind firmly on the task and regularly checking my reflection – or lack of reflection – in the windows of the stores I passed. I had just reached the food court marking the halfway point on my route when something stopped me in my tracks. Right in front of me stood Jake White, leaning against a table belonging to a coffee house and looking at his phone. Of course, there was nothing remarkable about that. Like me, Jake lived close by, and I would often see him around here at the weekend with his friends. Usually he would say "hey" if he saw me, and I would say "hey" back. Or sometimes I would go with "hi", to change it up a little. One time I even went for "hiyaaaa" but regretted it afterwards – it wasn't really me. Anyway, the point was, I often saw him around, so what was different this time? Well, a couple of things were different: number one, this time I was invisible. Number two... well, just between the two of us, I kind of liked it when he held my hand after the big football disaster on the playground. It felt kind of nice, okay? Nothing wrong with that.

Being invisible means you can look at a person for as long as you want without it being awkward. I stood and watched Jake for a couple of minutes as he scrolled through things on his phone, a smile flickering across his face every now and then when he saw something amusing. He had a nice smile. Warm. He was always a bit different from the other boys: more laid back, and quieter, but when he spoke people listened. I remembered some of our adventures together as small children, like going down a big slide together and getting stuck. Jake found it hilarious, and his sense of fun was infectious - the more people piled up behind us, the more we laughed. It was a long time ago now though... did he still see me as that little girl with a messy pony tail that never stayed in and an almost un-healthy obsession with penguins? Or did he see that I'd grown up, just like he had?

I cautiously stepped a little closer to him, then closer still, until he was no more than two feet away from me. I was close enough to see his chest slowly rising and falling with each breath. What was I planning on doing? A ripple of nervous energy passed through me, leaving every hair on my arms standing on end. I was close enough to lean forward and...

"JAKE!"

A girl's voice shattered the moment like a grand piano dropped on a thin pane of glass from a great height, and Jake's eyes flew up from his phone, pointing right in my direction. I turned and ran, casting aside all my usual precautions about tread-ing quietly and making sure I didn't bump into anyone. I sprinted out of the shopping centre at full speed and didn't stop until I was halfway home.

Pausing for breath, I found to my relief that I was still invisible – I had obviously kept my focus pretty well despite the moment of crisis back there.

What had I been thinking though? Was I going to kiss Jake? How would he, or indeed anyone, react to being kissed by an invisible person? I hadn't really thought that one through, I conceded with a shake of my head as I resumed my journey home at a more sensible walking pace. Drawing near my house, I was just starting to wonder who the girl was who had shouted Jake's name when I saw another of my neighbours, a boy called Oliver from the next street over. He was only eight years old or so, but he was actually not a bad kid, suitably respectful to people such as myself who had several more years of wisdom and experience.

Oliver had his skateboard with him, quite a nice one. I think he might have got it for Christmas. He was standing with one foot on the board and the other on the ground, talking to an older boy I vaguely recognised. As I got closer to them I realised that the older kid was Toby Brownlow, who had been expelled from my school for bullying maybe a year ago. He was a few years above me, probably sixteen or seventeen by now. When I got within earshot it became clear that their conversation was not a friendly one, and that Toby hadn't changed much since I last saw him.

"Just give me a quick lend of the board, yeah? I'm just gonna do a couple of tricks then give it right back, you get me?"

"But my mum says I can't lend it to anyone..."

"Mummy says I can't lend it to anyone," Toby sneered, in a very weak impression of Oliver's voice. "I don't care what Mummy says, just gimme the board, right now yeah, or else Mummy's gonna have more to worry about than just a missing skateboard."

I could see Oliver was desperately fighting back tears at the thought of losing his prized possession, but was on the point of surrendering it. What could I do? If there was ever a moment to use my powers for good, this was it, wasn't it? The question was, how exactly should I go about it? In the comics I'd read, the fight against crime involved a lot of punching people in the face. Usually, the people who were punched would immediately collapse on the floor, unconscious. Would that work here though? I doubted it. Sometimes my dad let me punch him if we were having a play-fight or something like that, and he didn't seem to even feel it. I looked down towards my small fists – a pointless activity as I was still invisible – and felt the futility of taking on Toby with them. He was quite tall, so apart from anything else I would have to jump to even reach his face with a punch. Dismissing that idea, I looked around for a weapon. A loose brick or a scaffolding pole would have been ideal, and you always see that sort of thing lying around, don't you? Well, not when you need one, it turns out. There was not a single thing within reach except for a few pebbles no larger than grapes, an empty cigarette packet, and a plastic recycling box sitting outside a nearby house.

Supressing a smile at the thought of a superhero using any of those items to take on a criminal mastermind, I decided I had to improvise. Toby had his back to me and by this time he had his hands on the board, trying to yank it free from Oliver's despairing grasp. I hurried towards them and crouched on the ground right behind Toby's legs. He gave a final heave, ripping the board from Oliver with a laugh of triumph. His laughter soon turned to a surprisingly high-pitched shriek of surprise however, as his momentum carried him backwards and he tumbled heavily over my invisible back in what I came to think of afterwards as a "Super Tabletop".

The skateboard flew out of his hands and into the road, where it nearly hit an oncoming car.

The driver slammed on his brakes and yelled at Toby, using every swear word I'd ever heard plus a few that were entirely new to me. The recipient of this abuse picked himself up and ran for it without looking back, probably a bit confused about what the hell had just happened to him. Oliver wandered into the road to retrieve his board but then just stood there holding it, oblivious of the oncoming traffic. I sighed inwardly – apparently a hero's work is never done. Stepping behind him I blinked back in, then grabbed his arm and pulled him out of harm's way.

"Come on kid, can't have you getting run over right in front of me – I'd never hear the end of it," I told him, though not unkindly. I could see he was suffering from the shock of the encounter with Toby, and he spent a moment looking at me, then his board, as if he'd never seen either before in his life. Then he threw his arm around my waist and hugged me, babbling some sort of expression of gratitude and admiration for what I'd done. I wasn't really sure if he somehow realised that I'd been the saviour of his skateboard or if he was just thanking me for not letting him get splatted all over the road by a rapidly approaching Skoda Fabia, but either way a thank you is always appreciated.

I patted him on the head and reassured him, "Any time you need help, the amazing Maddie Sykes is here for you." As soon as I'd said the words I regretted them: talking about myself in the third person? Seriously. Luckily he was still gibbering incoherently and may not have heard, so I gently prised him off and pointed him in the direction of home with some words of advice about being more careful in future, never talking to strangers, blah blah.

Despite the slightly mundane nature of the crime I'd prevented, I felt on top of the world as I strode home using my most confident power walk.

I'd foiled a criminal, saved an innocent child, and in doing so had truly become the world's first real-life superhero. Awesome.

Yep, there was no doubt about it, things were just going to get better and better from this point onwards.

11.

The next day was Sunday, and I woke up still feeling very positive after my heroics with Oliver. I lay in bed for a while and read some more of my book, but a modern-day thought kept intruding into the old-fashioned scenes of the story. I'd already been through it a hundred times, but I found myself feeling the urge to share my secret with my parents again. Perhaps in my upbeat frame of mind I was more inclined to believe they could help me.

Turning it over in my mind, I settled on the idea of confiding in my dad. He was more laid back than Mum, less likely to panic or get hysterical about the changes in me. Once I had him on my side, we could tackle Mum together… maybe. I'd see how he thought we should play it.

I was just pulling some clothes on when I heard the front door close. Looking out of my window, I saw Dad walking away from the house. Where was he going on his own on a Sunday morning? I decided to go after him and find out, maybe walk with him and take the opportunity to talk, if the moment seemed right. I raced downstairs and grabbed my shoes, then hesitated at the front door. I was feeling the urge to disappear again, but it didn't really make sense – I couldn't exactly have a normal conversation with him if he couldn't see me. After a moment of indecision, I changed my plan: I would follow him, invisibly, just to see what he was up to, and then decide whether it was a good moment to have the big discussion.

I blinked out, and rushed into the street outside. Luckily my dad does everything slowly, and that includes walking. He was still in view, maybe a hundred yards down the road, his hands in his pockets and his shoulders hunched up as he trudged on. I hurried after him, getting within twenty feet or so. Then I slowed to match his pace as he turned a corner and began to climb the hill that led towards Springwell Heights, one of the rougher areas of town.

This sparked all kinds of odd ideas in my mind. Why would Dad want or need to go there? Apart from a good Chinese restaurant, which would be closed at this time of day, the place had very little in the way of possible attractions. Did he have some kind of drug or gambling habit? Did he secretly come here all the time? As my thoughts darkened, the weather did the same. Thick banks of black clouds gathered above us as we made our way up the hill, heightening the sense that we were heading in the wrong direction. The breeze became a chill wind which seemed to cut straight through my thin clothes, and I regretted not having had time to grab a coat.

Within a few minutes we had reached the centre of Springwell Heights, as desolate a place as you could wish to see. Apart from my father there was barely a single living thing in view, just the ugly 1960s concrete boxes that passed for housing in this neighbourhood, litter blowing around and the occasional rat. The clouds got even thicker over our heads and seemed to loom down so low I could almost touch them. It became almost unnaturally dark, more like late evening than midmorning, and the wind cranked up another notch, but still our solitary journey continued. I found myself leaning forward into the gale just to maintain some momentum, as it numbed my face and tossed my hair in every direction. I had expected Dad to turn off here, perhaps to make his way towards the dodgy pub I knew was somewhere nearby, but he stuck to the main road and plodded on until we neared the gentle descent that marked the far side of this hellhole. Where could he be going? There wasn't anything for miles in this direction, not that I'd ever been along here before... or had I? As we left Springwell Heights I noticed a stunted tree in the strange shape of a man on horseback, and it seemed to trigger some vague and distant memory. When had I seen it before? A feeling of unease rose in my stomach, and at that moment the roaring wind dropped as abruptly as if a huge fan had been unplugged. As I paused in front of the tree, the sudden eerie silence felt almost deafening.

Despite the dim light, there was no mistaking the twisted branches and dark leaves in front of me. I must have come this way before. A hazy recollection seemed to dance just out of my reach, and I closed my eyes, trying to bring it to the surface. Something cold against my forehead... glass? Yes, of course – my face had been leaning against the window of the car, looking out. I'd seen the tree. Noticed its shape. I hadn't pointed it out to anyone though. Why not? Because something was wrong. Nobody was speaking. And there was pain… terrible pain…

I opened my eyes with a jolt.

I didn't want to think about that.

Where was Dad? He'd disappeared – but a cold sense of certainty gripped me, a feeling that I knew where he'd gone and why. I fought back the feeling, but an unknown force seemed to take control of my feet and drag me forward, towards a turning just a little further down the hill. When I reached the turning I saw it was an entrance, an open metal gate with a sign on it, a name of some sort. I didn't read it, didn't want to know what this place was, but I already knew. I'd been here before.

The clouds gave a distant rumble as I advanced, each step more difficult than the last. Peering into the gloom I made out Dad, just up ahead. There was nobody else there, and my foot-steps crunched loudly on the gravel path, but Dad never looked around. He was kneeling on the muddy ground, his head in his hands. Kneeling in front of something – what was it? I knew what it was. A headstone. A grave.

My legs turned to jelly and I fell forwards, face down in the grass beside the path. I wanted to just lie there, to never get up again, but I had to see for myself what was written on that headstone. I tried to stand but my legs wouldn't respond, so I dragged myself forward with my hands, through the grass, through the mud, towards my father.

As I hauled myself close to him there was an explosion of thunder so loud it seemed to rattle every bone in my body, and the storm finally broke above us. Ice-cold rain lashed over me, hitting the soft ground so hard it left little indentations in the mud. My hair was in my eyes, stuck to my face by a mixture of mud and rain, and I felt a strong urge to leave it there so I couldn't see what was now in front of me – but I knew I had to see it. With difficulty I scraped my hair back, wiped the mud from my eyes, and read.

IN LOVING MEMORY OF

ANNA SYKES

BELOVED WIFE OF PETER

AND MOTHER OF MADELINE

12.

Mum.

It was Mum's grave.

I rolled over on my back and closed my eyes as the wind and rain tore at my flesh. This was crazy. Mum wasn't dead – I'd seen her... when exactly? Yesterday? No, nobody was in when I got home, and I'd stayed in my room all night. Surely the day before though?

I racked my brain, suddenly feeling as though there was an important memory I had buried somewhere, far out of reach. When did I last see

Mum? I pictured her in my mind, with her long red curls cascading down her back and her favourite yellow scarf around her neck. Memories of us together played out one after the other like a slideshow: running around on the beach when I was maybe three or four, Mum and Dad laughing when I got scared of a crab. Then getting dropped off for my first day of school, my parents trying not to cry as they waved me off from the gates. A school Christmas play when I was seven, with me in the prestigious role of Donkey, Mum and Dad in the audience almost bursting with pride when I sang my solo.

This was no good – I had to go forward, closer to the present day, much as I didn't want to. With an effort I picture myself at maybe twelve years old, sitting on the stairs in our house with my hands over my ears as my parents yelled at each other in the kitchen. Next I was thirteen, wishing a hole in the ground would swallow me up as Mum took offence at something Dad had said and stormed out of a restaurant, slamming the door so hard it made the other customers jump.

And then – there was something missing. I felt as if I was swimming through the warm water near the surface of the sea, sunlight dancing off all my memories as they floated around me. It was beautiful up here, and I wanted to float here forever, but something made me look down. In the depths of the ocean below me there was hardly any light, and it was cold, so cold. Was there something down there? I screwed up my eyes, and thought I saw something moving – something dark and ugly.

I didn't want to go down there in the dismal depths of the water, but I had to. I took a deep breath and dived, pulling myself downwards. With every moment I descended, the light faded and the temperature dropped. My arms felt numb and heavy as I thrust them out in front of me and dragged myself forward through the increasingly murky water.

What was I swimming towards? At first I thought it was some nightmarish sea monster that was waiting to devour me at my journey's end, but I became aware of a metallic clanking noise as I got closer to it. Some sort of machine, perhaps? A steel trap that would close around me and imprison me down here forever?

At last, with a final desperate thrust, I was floating next to the mysterious object and saw it clearly for the first time. It was nothing like the sinister things I had imagined – in fact it could hardly have been less terrifying. Gently bobbing in the water before me was a small wooden chest, a chest that was very familiar to me. It had once contained Mahjong pieces, but when I was a little girl I liked it so much that my dad had emptied it out and given it to me. Ever since then it had stood on the dressing table in my room and had contained various things as I grew up: first little plastic animals, then tiny squishy Disney characters, then makeup, and most recently keepsakes – tickets for events I'd been to, photos, and other little mementos.

What was inside it now? It was wrapped in rusty chains which trailed off into the depths below, preventing it from floating to the surface. The chains were fastened with a padlock, but to my surprise I found that I held the key in my hand. I grabbed the lock and as I inserted the key, with some difficulty, I noticed something written on the chest, in my own handwriting. Just one word.

NO!

I hesitated, but only for a second. "Sorry, Maddie, but I think I have to open this now," I told myself. I twisted the key in the lock and the chains fell away leaving me with the box in my hands, which shook slightly as I carefully opened the lid and looked inside.

It was almost empty. There was just one thing in there, lying quite innocently at the bottom of the chest. It was a phone. A phone with a white face, and a plastic cover decorated with pictures of dogs wearing top hats. Mum's phone.

Why did I have Mum's phone, and why was it down here?

The memory hit me like a lightning bolt, and I dropped the chest as my whole body convulsed in pain. A new scene from the recent past played out in my mind, the images so bright and sharply defined that I felt as though they were being burned into my brain.

I was at home. It was just me and Mum. She was in the kitchen. I was watching TV.

My phone was dead, but I wanted to check something online. Her phone was in her bag, hanging over the back of a chair. I grabbed it and hit the home button. It asked me for a passcode. I didn't know her code, but I tried the same one she had suggested I use on mine, my birth date. It worked, first time. I remember laughing, and calling out to Mum that she really should be more careful. She didn't hear me.

I saw she had a message. It didn't have a proper name against it, just "M, Work". I looked at the message. It was… oh my god, it was bad, it was… romantic. Serious, full-on romance.

"Mum…?" I called, but my voice came out in a weird, muffled whimper, and again she didn't hear me.

I looked at the message history, and there were dozens of messages like that from "M, Work". Not just messages from him though, messages sent to him as well, messages Mum had sent, and they were just as bad. Maybe worse.

I went through the hall and stood in the kitchen doorway. Mum was making dinner. Her curly red hair was tied back in a ponytail, like she always had it if she was cooking or going to the gym. I held up the phone and said, "Mum."

She turned around, smiling – but her expression changed when she saw my face and then saw her phone in my hand. She took a step forwards but I backed away. "Maddie," she said, keeping her voice icy calm, "give me my phone right now please."

"No!" I shouted. "I'm showing it to Dad!"

"Maddie, just calm down and let's talk about this sensibly. Give me the phone."

"No!" I screamed again, and as she moved towards me I turned and ran down the hall, throwing open the front door and bursting through it onto our driveway.

"Maddie, come back here this instant!" Mum yelled, following me outside. Neither of us even had our shoes on, but I had to get away, I couldn't stay there and talk about this, I couldn't let her catch me. I ran out into the street.

"Maddie!" Mum shouted again, running after me. Then I heard the squeal of tires on the wet road, and *the sickening thud of a vehicle colliding with something at speed.*

Mum.

13.

Suddenly I felt myself being pulled upwards from the depths into which I'd plunged. I opened my eyes and saw that Dad had picked me up off the muddy ground and was carrying me across the cemetery towards the shelter of a large tree. He didn't say anything until he'd put me down on the ground, sitting with my back against the broad trunk of the tree, and wiped some of the mud off my face.

"Jesus, Maddie, you look terrible. What were you thinking, coming out in this weather wearing just a t-shirt? And aren't these your pyjama bottoms?"

I looked down. They were indeed. My pink, fluffy pyjama bottoms with unicorns on. I bought them to be ironic but they were secretly my favourites. They were looking a lot less pink and fluffy now, and a lot more brown and ragged. I hadn't realised I was still wearing them. I didn't know what to say, so I waited for Dad to say something.

"Look, Maddie..." he resumed after a long pause, clearly struggling to choose the right words, "I'm sorry. You've really been through it, and I haven't been there for you. I've been... well, you know, this has all been..."

He trailed off and waved an arm vaguely in the direction of Mum's grave, barely visible through the curtain of rain that continued to bombard the world beyond the protective arms of the tree above us.

"I know," I answered. "It's okay."

"No, it's not okay, I've been so wrapped up in my own grief that I didn't stop to think how you were feeling. I didn't see how you were hurting, how much weight you've lost, how you haven't been sleeping, any of it. Well, that ends today. In fact, it ended yesterday afternoon. I told myself I'd just come here one last time on my own, to say good-bye, and then focus on putting you first and helping you in any way I can. I just... I'm so sorry..."

His eyes filled with tears and he quickly rubbed his shirt-sleeve across his face to dry them. I'd never seen him cry. The tears looked ridiculously out of place in his eyes, like lobsters on a tennis court, and he turned away for a moment so I wouldn't see them.

"Dad, honestly, it's okay. None of this is your fault."

He turned back to me and took my hand.

"Maddie, there's something really important I have to tell you. I read your diary. Yesterday. While you were out. That's what opened my eyes to how selfish I've been and how much more support I need to give you. And – please believe me when I say this – *you are not invisible."*

Not invisible. The words sounded ridiculous, I'd become so used to thinking of invisibility as one of my defining qualities. For a moment I thought he was just speaking metaphorically, but no – he'd read my diary from cover to cover, with all that detailed analysis of my power: how I'd used it, how I'd practised with it, how it had let me down on occasion and all the problems it had caused. He knew about everything, from my stupid theft of the mints from Mrs Rai to the even stupider moment where I tried to kiss Jake.

Thing was, he had an explanation for all of it. He said if there were times at home when he didn't seem to see me, it was just because he was lost in his own thoughts, struggling to cope. He said that sometimes it was hard to look at me, because I reminded him of Mum.

He suggested that if Lucy sometimes acted like she didn't see me, that was because people feel awkward around friends who have suffered a loss, and they don't know what to say. He said that was especially true if people know you were actually there when something terrible happened. He didn't say what I was thinking, "People feel awkward when they know it was all your fault, that your mum died because of you." He said that it was an accident, that nobody was to blame.

He'd spoken to Mrs Rai, and to my teachers, and even to Jake White. They all said they'd noticed me acting strangely. Dad thought they had probably seen me creeping around, believing myself to be invisible, when all the time I was in plain view. He said my teachers had been going easy on me because of Mum, and that's why they hadn't really picked me up on it.

He showed me a picture of myself from a month ago, before Mum died, and another picture from yesterday, taken without me noticing. I was shocked at the difference: that shyly smiling girl with everything going for her had been replaced by a zombie with lank, greasy hair, dark circles around her red eyes, and skin that was deathly pale. I wasn't well, Dad explained. I'd had a huge shock, and my brain had created this whole invisibility fantasy as a way of protecting me from reality. He said he would help me, take me to bereavement counselling, so we could get through this together.

My mind was spinning. The way Dad talked about everything that had been happening to me kind of made sense, but I couldn't think about all that just then. I couldn't think about anything except the fact that Mum was gone and I would never see her again. The dam burst at that moment, and I cried – I cried so hard I found myself fighting for breath. I stood up and put my arms around Dad, and cried some more. Eventually, when I had no more tears left, I looked out at the graveyard beyond our protective tree and found the rain had stopped. Faint rays of sunlight were filtering through the storm clouds as they broke apart, and the brightest of these fell on Mum's grave. I could see it clearly for the first time, and it felt okay if people could see me too.

Maybe my invisibility really was just a protective cloak I'd created in my mind to protect me from all the pain and guilt. And maybe I didn't need to be the amazing Maddie Sykes any more. Maybe I should just be plain Maddie, like before.

Maybe.

14.

I didn't think much about being invisible over the next few weeks. I was getting used to the idea that Mum was gone, and trying to convince myself that it wasn't my fault. My dad helped as much as he could, and in doing so it seemed like he started to come to terms with the tragedy himself. He took me to see a counsellor, and although she didn't say that much she was a great listener. I spent hours talking to her about Mum, my memories of her, and all my strange experiences since she died. Eventually I began to feel, if not exactly better about life, at least more able to cope and carry on.

One of the first things I had done when we came back from the cemetery that day was to get rid of Mum's phone. It was in my room, inside the Mahjong box just as I'd pictured it. I took it to the park and threw it in the river; for some reason that made me feel like a great weight had lifted from my shoulders. I never showed it to Dad, never even told him I had it. He never knew why I had argued with Mum that day, or why I was running away from her when the accident happened. I didn't see any point in telling him the truth, it would only make him feel worse.

As the weeks went by and I began to get better at dealing with our loss, eventually my thoughts turned back to the time when I thought I was invisible. My counsellor had urged me not to spend too much time dwelling on that subject, but I suppose it was inevitable. Despite all Dad's logical explanations, a part of me still wondered if it really was all in my imagination. I tried blinking out a couple of times just out of curiosity, without any real belief that it would work, and sure enough it didn't. Eventually I dismissed it from my mind, just as my counsellor suggested. It was the sensible thing to do, leaving all of that behind me and moving on.

One night, maybe two months after that day in the graveyard, I was in bed, getting my thoughts in order before falling asleep. I was just going over my plans for the coming week when a blinding thought suddenly struck me like a thunderbolt.

In the shopping centre that time. In the bathrooms. I turned invisible. I opened the door of the cubicle and that woman charged straight in without giving me a chance to leave. She must not have seen me... but I was standing right there. If I wasn't invisible, it didn't make sense, did it? Not unless she was some kind of lunatic who didn't understand that toilet cubicles weren't for sharing.

Sitting up in bed, I flicked on my bedside light with trembling hands. I tried to blink out, but nothing happened.

"It's been a while," I reminded myself, "I could just be a bit rusty. Slow it down."

I took it right back to basics, back to how it all began. I concentrated hard, imagining a gradual transition to invisibility that started at my feet and worked its way up.

Nothing.

Wait… did my fingers have that glassy shimmer, just for a second? Just the faintest hint of transparency?

I closed my eyes, took a deep breath, and disappeared.

THE END

THANK YOU for reading The Amazing Maddie Sykes!

If you enjoyed Maddie's adventures, it would mean a lot to me if you could take a moment to leave a rating on Amazon, GoodReads or social media. Independent authors like me depend on our readers to help get the word out about our books, and just a few kind words can make a huge difference.

Until the next time - happy reading!

~Linton~

www.LintonDarling.com

@LintonDarling

Also by Linton Darling

Mischief, mystery and danger - can Maya Madison es-cape from Siberia, saving herself, her friends and a baby wolf?

LOST SNOWFLAKES – Available now

Made in the USA
Middletown, DE
20 March 2020

86958170R00106